The Gods in Our Eyes

M D FORTIER

To my parents, who now get to say:

"Look, our son wrote a book!"

And to Heather & Audrey, who both read this and didn't tell me to toss it in a canal

THE GODS IN OUR EYES

~ One ~

"Ours is an Infinite Quest, from the Dawn of Man until Oblivion, to gather the collective knowledge of Existence."

Seyj Maarthin,
First Recordant of Encodyn

The first moon had risen over the opalescent sands of Arc as Reader Entrant Aeryn Anno exited the grand parlor of his region's Temple entrance. He drew in his first breath of fresh air in nearly seven of the Greater Moon's orbits. It felt like the breath of Life itself.

Aeryn strode down the stonework path, descending in sequences of stairs and sloping road towards the common grounds of the small residential below. There was a crisp breeze; a welcome change from the stillness of the underground catacombs where Aeryn spent most of his service to the Records. He would savor every moment of it.

The Residential was a feat timeless practicality. A few sandstone benches lined the long sides of the sparse courtyard: an octagonal space with a modest fountain to serve as its centerpiece. The Reader took a seat, admiring the company of celestials above. Calling them "moons" would be a disservice to their reality. This was a system unique to itself in the vast cosmos, with each piece meticulously collected.

Just as its cosmic comrades were not native to this system, the Opal Moon itself came to inhabit it from a distant galaxy. It was built to observe the destruction of the Twin Planets Yr and Ang, and when that didn't happen, it became the site of the most expansive database of knowledge in the universe: The Records of All & Everything.

The Records are an ever-expanding database of sentient activity, from the glyphic attempts at communication of prehistory to the almost-present. Its breadth of knowledge has served as the standard for intragalactic knowledge for time immemorable.

Other Readers were already gathering amongst themselves or heading to the pantry hall to break their fasts for the evening. Aeryn would wait for the initial rush to subside. He wasn't in any hurry to be back indoors.

Meals were modest but always enjoyable. The goodwill of those who plied their trade nearby, as well as the steady flow of benefactor care packages kept the kitchens stocked with all manner of spices, meats, and vegetation. His nose twisted at a scent reminiscent of loamy soil and pungent greens meant that the Culinaires had prepared a stew of cultured asteroid fungus with kelps and amphibiads from a nearby marsh planet.

Aeryn would dive into that momentarily. For now, his gaze met that of an approaching figure. It was a Speaker, recognizable from the necklace it wore; a thin bronze chain adorned with a pendant depicting a sphere inside a V-shaped cone, the universal symbol for "voice."

It was the symbol of their sect: those whose charge was to travel between the Opal Moon and those planets that have yet to join the Records. Or, in some cases, that have yet to accept its invitations.

"Look who's back on the surface," said the figure. There was an eerie familiarity between the long-necked, golden-scaled Hissari before him and an Earthen reptile, though no analysis of either revealed any genetic overlap. Even our comparative genetic structures differ enough that the phenotypical coincidence is astounding.

"My first night out, and I see both this beautiful moonrise, and my closest friend," Aeryn replied. "And welcome home to you, Sip. How were the Records received in the Penheral system?"

Sip sighed the weighted sigh of one left with only their breath to carry. Aeryn braced for bad news.

"In the main cities, we were mostly well received. Outside them, it seems the truth falls on closed ears."

He turned his head toward the horizon. The third moon was just peeking over it.

"Still, there were some that were willing. I do wish that willingness was more pervasive."

Aeryn shifted in his seat, motioning for the Speaker to sit.

"This dismay in your voice is palpable," Aeryn said. "We can only do our small parts, not much more. If we enlighten any towards accepting the Records as part of their lives, we have done no more than if we had not. Maarthin himself said that."

"The old Seyja said a lot of things," Sip replied. "Your optimism is your most amenable flaw. I worry for those who create their own false truths."

He closed his marble eyes for an extended moment, then flashed a toothy smile.

"Forget about it, I don't mean to burden you with Speaker troubles. Have you eaten? I smelled amphibiads the moment our ship opened the hatches."

He knew the small, rotund creatures were a staple of Hissari diets, and Sip was looking ravenous in anticipation.

"I haven't yet," said Aeryn, smiling wide, "And remember: your burdens are mine as well, and they're no match for the pair of us. We should get to the hall before we miss the feast."

They departed for the refectory, recalling previous meals and issuing challenges concerning how much dessert one could possibly consume. Outside the entrance, the pair ran into Axly and Luc, two other Record Keepers (colloquially known as "Arkays"). Axly was a Reader, like Aeryn, and Luc was a Speaker. Sip knew him better than Aeryn did, having been offworld together many times, and Aeryn hadn't come around to him just yet. He was a nice enough guy, and very smart, but he was too handsome. Boys who grow up knowing they're handsome have personalities that Aeryn described as "lacking." Axly liked him a great deal. The two were talking to a distinguished looking, very pale individual.

Aeryn recognized the third person as Blaike Irrus, a hyumin zynoid, custom-fathered by Glynn Irrus, the head of the Irrus Group as his daughter and successor. She was here as part of her education, as some of the temporary residents are, but showed so much talent for organizing and utilizing data that she was asked to stay and help improve existing systems. Much to the chagrin of her stem-father, she agreed to a decade of service.

The group went inside and collected trays of food, then returned outside to conglomerate at their usual table on the eastern outskirts of the plaza. There was a pleasant chill on the wind.

"Any word about when the ships are arriving?" Sip asked no one in particular.

"OO!" blurted Axly, mouth halfway full. She chomped down the stew then replied, "Yes! She's coming home tonight! It should be anytime now."

The "she" to whom Axly referred was her sister, Sha'an. Aeryn had been in love with Sha'an since the day he met her.

It had been the morning of his first weekend on the Opal Moon, brand new to the academy, and lost in the crowd. He sat in a corner with his handheld device, ignoring the hubbub around him, when a shadow fell across his screen. He looked up, and in the light of the sunrise saw the most beautiful face he had ever seen. Maybe it was how the sun cast a glimmer of gold across her face, her radiant smile, or the fact that she was talking to him at all; he was enraptured.

"Whatcha playing?" she asked.

It took Aeryn a moment to respond. He hadn't talked to anyone yet that morning and his voice caught in his throat.

*"It -**cough**—it's the new Endless Journey game," he managed.*

She sat down next to him. "Oh! I heard it's better than the last entry. They really missed the mark on that one. The whole thing felt like a car ride with random battles."

Aeryn's eyes lit up. "It was! This one is so much better. It really goes back to the roots of the series."

She held out her hand. "I'm Sha'an."

He took it and responded, "Aeryn. Well met, Sha'an."

And the rest, as they say, is history.

"I'm sad I'll be gone before I get to see her. My ship is leaving right after refections," said Luc.

"Very unfortunate," chimed Aeryn. He couldn't help but grin and turned towards the refectory. "Shall we for seconds?"

"Always," replied Sip.

After many helpings of stew, the group said their farewells outside the entrance. Sip let out a gratified belch. He seemed pleased with himself.

"Anyone for a round in the Aug room? Knock off a few of these," he asked, patting his many food-based lumps.

"You spend too much time playing games in there," said Blaike. "If you spent half the time you did in there practicing your speeches, you'd be a Speaker Adept by now."

Sip shrugged, or his version of shrugging.

"You're missing the point. I now have valuable skills pertinent to offworld survival."

The group's synchronized guffaw was audible through the square.

"And what skills are those?" Blaike laughed. "Everything in those games is rot from barbaric times. I don't know why they keep them around."

"She's right," chimed Axly. "It's all fighting and hero-fantasy. These 'skills' aren't made for this age."

Sip groaned. "They're not some bygone thing! Look what happened to the Ta'ak; what a mess. Second most advanced civilization in the stars, torn to bits by inner turmoil."

He looked to Aeryn for agreement.

Aeryn shrugged. "I'm not sure what happened to the Ta'ak, but I do know that the games are fun. Whether or not we ever need these skills is out of my purview."

Luc laughed. "Aeryn, you spend almost as much time as Sip does in there. I'm surprised you're not itching for a round after being under for so long."

Ugh, thought Aeryn. Everything Luc said felt backhanded.

"He does not," said Axly. "Aeryn is the best tutor on the whole moon. He's always in one study room or another helping someone."

"That 'someone' being you?" retorted Luc.

Blaike's stare bored into the back of his head. He must have felt it.

"...always good to have a friend like that," he offered, then slunk his head.

Axly closed the distance between herself and Aeryn. She squished his cheeks.

"He's not the hero type. He doesn't need to be."

The group dispersed at the juncture between sleeping quarters. Sip meandered back towards his encampment; his midsection engorged from his exuberant eating. Everyone had the option of sleeping where they please, but Sip chose to make his outside dwelling more permanent. Others had soon followed suit. Sip had quite the following.

Aeryn had been underground for so long; it seemed a waste of such a visage of an evening to retire already. The third moon was passing overhead, parallel in path to the horizon, a smaller but much closer phenomenon: The Moon so aptly named Precipice.

This moon was in perfect orbit; not slowly leaving or falling, always on the razor-edge of both. The motion of this satellite was the basis for the passage of days on the planet, and for the records kept therein. It was also the calendar day for Universal Recorded Time, used by starfaring vessels across the cosmos.

It could seem strange to base such a vast measurement system on so specific a location, but the similarity to the timing of Earth's rotation made it an attractive parallel for hyumin explorers. The Records were, of course, a hyumin invention, set up by the First of Us to prevent the loss of the history of Life. Given the history of the loss of history, it was their first prerogative when the Earthen Diaspora scattered our forebears to the stars to ensure that we never forget who we once were and where our origins lie. *The ego,* thought Aeryn, visibly chuckling to himself.

"He's not the hero type"

For some reason, that thought kept going through his head. He sat upon the same bench and watched the dance of the orbitals entertaining the night sky into its lulls, until the stardust overtook his eyes. He slept a dreamless sleep of one unburdened.

It would be his last for some time.

~ Two ~

"Tragedy is never on time. It is often too early, sometimes too late, and bears only the one, melancholic gift."

Seyj Hangrof the Joyous

A thunderous rumble awoke the young Reader, startling him from his slumber. In the distance, he could see an immense passenger star-cruiser on the landing pad. The force of its landing engines created a sound like the beating of barrel-drums, cascading the dunes of glass sand around it.

"Strange," he blurted out, to no one in particular. It was already morning. Other recordants were also looking at the ship, seemingly just as puzzled as he. He felt a twinge of reassurance at this, in that he had expected this ship much earlier. Sip tapped him on the shoulder as he passed by. Aeryn splashed his face with water from the fountain and followed. The star shone through the Twins as if it too could not believe the sight, focused as it was.

As he got closer, Aeryn noticed the ship's hull was battered in places, hulls pierced. Behind its mass were a handful of other ships in similar condition.

Then he saw something that narrowed his focus to a pinhole. There was nothing else: no ship, no sandals falling off, no crowd of confused onlookers; nothing but Aeryn and a face.

The face was one he knew fondly. The face was the one he'd laughed with, made promises to, even kissed once. The face was Sha 'an, and hers was the face of pain. Aeryn crashed past medical personnel and equipment. He was only pulled from his trance by the cords tripping him underfoot. He narrowly averted a rolling lamp when he arrived at her transport cot, fully out of breath. The friend he knew was still there, though the years that separated them had brought Sha' an closer to the form of adulthood; her face more lined and touched by Life. But that wasn't what he noticed.

Bruises, Aeryn thought. *What...how...who did this? Who? And why? And WHY?!* His brain raced a million horrific scenarios against one another. Settling on one to accept seemed worse than the barrage. There were patches of dried blood around her nose and mouth, and a deep ring of bruising on her throat. One of her ears was cuffed and her hair was ripped near the back. Whoever had done this, they weren't of any sane state. *Who?*

"Ae..."

A single syllable in which all the power in the universe could have been kept. One word that brought Aeryn from the brink of despair to the pinnacle of happiness. His weeping smile must have looked just short of madness.

"Sha'an," he stammered through welling tears, "You're hurt."

The words were barely out of his mouth when the sadness was replaced with rage. The sharp, metallic taste of blood rushed to his tongue.

"Who did this? what happened?"

Sha'an turned her head with such effort, Aeryn felt it in his bones. A wisp of a word escaped her cracked lips.

" ... home..."

A member of the medical staff approached. It was a zynoid, like Blaike, but not the same; this was also a bioengineered being composed mostly of organic synthetics, combined with miles of nanoscopic wiring and bio-interactive circuits. They were often grown to resemble the biological traits of their fabricators, leading to a variety just as diverse as the populations they represented. They didn't have to, though. Some zynoids are pets, some livestock, some even living ships and weapons.

Aeryn shook the thought from his head. The zynoid bid him step aside while it took readings and switched out intravenous fluids. This particular zynoid was a specialized medical varietal whose hyuminoid likeness ended at its large, almondine head, wrapped in translucent white flesh, and sporting an extra set of arms, most likely inspired by their close allies, the Rrelt.

Shan's breathing was labored. She opened her eyes and smiled a brief, pained smile. "I didn't think I'd get to see you again, Anno," she said wearily. "It was..."

She trailed off and slumped over.

A machine beeped with increasing frequency, causing the zynoid medic to reappear and administer some kind of solution. the machine, and Sha'an, seemed to respond positively to this, though she did not wake. The medic looked at Aeryn, wordlessly put its hand on his shoulder, and smiled. It had a genuine look of empathy on its face, and Aeryn wondered if it had ever experienced loss. *Could it?* The zynoid brain was as complex as any biological one but could be tweaked to contain or expand certain aspects, to the preference of their handlers. Zynoids are in many ways just as much the people they were designed to look like, but they are considered para-sentient artificial intelligence and are therefore registered like property by their handlers. some cultures recognize those created to be children to their handlers as beings equal to themselves, like Blaike, though these are not the majority. On Arc, many of these children find happiness.

"Aer..I..." Aeryn snapped out of his thought. these intrusive thoughts happened at the worst times. He looked at her and tried to smile. She took a slow, deep breath, then spoke:

"They killed our host families. Not gracefully, not with show. Almost... predatory." she looked away, shedding a single river of tears. "I escaped because we were warned, but right outside the harbor..." she went silent, the river of tears becoming a torrent.

"They hate us. They say we caused their problems, that we ARE the problem."

She paused a moment then murmured, "I'm not a problem." Her breathing was labored.

"They weren't always like this," she gazed into the middle distance, looking for something. "Something changed."

Aeryn took her hand and held it firmly. He was about to speak when –

"Aeryn!"

It was Sip, running towards them. Or, what the equivalent to running is for Hissari. His dual tails moved in a way that was reminiscent of bipedalism, though anatomically, it was upright slithering. His face was locked in an expression of shock, his vent flaps like shutters in a windstorm.

“I came as quickly as I could!” He looked down to see Sha’an. Terror swept over his face, then he snapped back to Aeryn.

"All the outbound ships have been grounded. The closest off-world ships have been directed to return to safe harbor as well. What's going on? Did she say anything?" Aeryn knew that he meant well but was in no mind to recount the tale.

"It's worse out there than we thought, Sip," he managed. He paused a moment, his eyes never leaving Sha’an's face. "Much worse. And I'm going to find out why.”

Sip put his clawed hand on Sha'an's brow, saying a few lines in his ancestral language. "She's cold. By your warm blood standards, I mean."

He reached into his robe and produced a pair of dried, spherical amphibiads stretched across skewers.

"Have you eaten yet, Anno?" He said, extending his snack-holding hand. "I grabbed these off-world, have you tried them? They're so flavorful that..."

Sip must have remembered where he was, because he trailed off. "Anyway, you need to eat." Aeryn took one, biting into it halfheartedly. Sip was right, it was amazing, but against the context of his battered friend, he couldn't enjoy it.

Sha'an had been put in intensive care in the nearby Restorial, while Aeryn and Sip ambled down a road outside the cluster of buildings around the Records Hall entrance. The roads were lit with bio-luminal pavers that responded in waves of glistening color to the footsteps of its travelers. Occasionally one would come across long benches umbrellaed by a crystalline structure that would catch the moonlight and refract it below. The pair stopped at one such oasis. They sat in silence for a while. There were others at the rest stop: an older hyumin bearing the badge of a Speaker: a group of newly recruited students giggly about something; in the far corner, a young couple, clearly very in love and showing no shame in displaying it. Aeryn couldn't help but stare. Sha'an and he hadn't been in a romantic partnership, though he often thought she would be the only one he would think to have one with. It wasn't until he realized they were staring back at him that he turned away, ears and cheeks flushed with embarrassment. He turned back to Sip, who was stifling a laugh. *Nice to see him smiling, even if it is at my expense.*

Sip unfurled a node on his wristlet. Light danced upwards out of it into a scene depicting a hyumin man standing behind a podium. He was flanked by several robust men, mostly hyumin, and notably one Ta'ak. It was then that Aeryn noticed that they were all wearing at least one piece of a dark purple crystal.

That's weird, thought Aeryn. Ta'ak rarely venture off-planet these days, let alone serve employ to other species on other planets. They barely even came here.

The Ta'ak were one of the first civilizations encountered by hyumins, and a part of the Initial Consortium of Knowledge. Since then, though, relations have thinned. The Ta'ak had officially deactivated their search for knowledge, which is the closest act to leaving the Consortium since its inception. The Rrelt manage what little is left of Ta'ak Record Keeping tech but have mostly assimilated their own machines into Ta'ak territory.

The man at the podium was railing on against "foreign ideas" and the Record Keepers' presence on the planet. The crowd was responsive to his cries for their removal, becoming rowdier by the sentence.

Aeryn crinkled his brow. "Lots of planets take issue with some part of the Records or another. It almost always has to do with their native religions. What about this time caused them to turn violent?"

He couldn't fathom what would make them turn on the Arcays so quickly. They were part of the Records Network, they shouldn't be this reactionary.

"This is what he's usually like, but just recently, it got much worse." Sip gestured and the image changed. "Trauma alert; this isn't easy to watch."

The recording was shaky, probably filmed on a personal screen. When it came into focus, Aeryn gasped. The screen showed a mob of hyumins surrounding a zynoid boy, only distinguishable from a natural hyumin by his poreless skin and the Cera-port near the top of his spine. They were throwing bottles at him. One found its mark, causing purple fluid indicative of a hyumin-type zyn to pour down his head and neck. The crowd was yelling so loud you could barely hear the boy crying out. One person broke through the inner circle and swung a metal pipe at its head. There was a loud CRACK, and it went silent.

Then the mob descended, indistinguishable from a pack of predators upon their prey. The madness was interrupted by a bright flash and another BANG, then the video abruptly ended, pausing on a still of what remained of the zyn. One of its eyes had found the camera. It stared at them.

Sip flipped his wristlet closed. His body shook like a rattle.

"Disgusting. I wonder if it's like that on other planets. There hasn't been a full recall since..."

"Since before there was a 'y' in 'hyumin,'" Aeryn finished for him.

The two looked at each other for a moment. Sip cracked awkward grin. It was the only thing they could do to dispel the tension.

"That long?" Sip retorted. "Maybe you're right. Maybe we're living in another Age of Tumult. Or maybe this is a singular event, but I fully doubt that."

Most of the other travelers had left the rest stop. The last light of the Grand Moon was quickly fading; a sliver of hope, or its last vestige.

The two set out back to the residential, not speaking for much of the time. Aeryn was lost in his own thoughts, and Sip was lost in the stars. His pre-speaking hissing broke the silence.

"So much beauty," he said.

Aeryn looked up. The stars shown with unnatural intensity. Some nights, you could rediscover the stars, as if they'd never existed until this moment. This was one of those nights.

The journey back seemed to pass in an instant. Sip split off towards the bathing rooms, leaving Aeryn with his thoughts. He wouldn't be able to sleep like this, so he clicked on the sleep aid feature of his cuff and laid back on his pillow. His eyes darted back and forth between the corners of objects in his room. It was part of a mental game he made up early in life to pass the time, and now he couldn't help but do it. He had covered nearly half the room when he saw lights outside.

Aeryn leapt from the bed to the window. A cluster of gleaming circles near the harbor could only mean one thing: more unexpected ships. More evacuations. More Arcays hurt. He sat at the window, staring out as people in the harbor moved like ants in a line to unload the new ships. Aeryn watched the patterns of the figures until his eyes could no longer find purchase. He drifted off into a dreamless sleep.

Almost dreamless. For a moment, he felt conscious in the dark. He couldn't see anything, but he could feel the unmistakable presence of something out there.

Something that was watching.

~ Three ~

"Find forgiveness in yourself, then let go."

Promnus Jyulya Kreshin

A cold wind on lingering sweat interrupted his slumber. He had passed out on the sill, and his head hurt. *How old am I?* he thought wistfully. The pain had almost made him forget about the impending crisis. And Sha'an.

A twinge of fear gripped him in place. Held him from foot to heart and stifled his breathing.

"Aeryn!"

The voice freed him from his paralysis. It was Axly.

"Are you okay? You looked like a statue," she asked.

"I'm fine," he lied.

It was as much as he wanted to admit to her. She was a Reader Protus, the first level of Reader, and still spent most of her days in tutelage. After leaving the academy and becoming a Reader Entrant, one could be assigned to any corner of the Opal Moon, and they were lucky to have been assigned to the same area. Besides the Speakers assigned to them, they were most of each other's social lives. The assignments had brought Sip and Luc into their lives.

She was looking at him, one eyebrow raised. "Fine?"

"I'm sorry," he continued. "Weird night. What's going on? Have you seen your sister?"

Axly nodded. "She's in low shape, but tall spirits." She paused. "She asked for you."

Aeryn's ears perked at the words.

"Should I go now?"

She nodded. "Bring her a crystal bloom. She'll like that." She turned to leave, then doubled back. "And don't tell her I told you to. Oh, and go bathe. You reek like you're about to spoil."

Aeryn hadn't had a real bathing in a few days. He headed down to the basin-rooms adjacent the entrance to his apartments. Sip was there, slithering in the water with the haphazard joy of a much younger being. *He always finds the fun in everything.*

Seeing Aeryn, Sip popped his head above water, bobbling like a buoy.

"There you are, Anno, and about time. Did Axly come by? I ran into her on my way down here. She was looking for you."

Aeryn disrobed and plunged into the nearest single-occupant basin. He tossed back his hair and breathed a heavy sigh.

"She did. I'm heading to see Sha'an after this." He turned to face Sip. "Are you busy? Can you come?"

Sip rattled his head.

"Totally free. No outbound ships until we know more about these attacks." His voice had lowered. "I'm thinking this is a much bigger problem than we know. Like these are just the ominous beginnings."

He perked up again, in his usual indomitable fashion.

"We're lucky to be living in such interesting times. It can get a little boring around here. Not to complain about peace, but maybe they could bring a rodeo show around every so often?"

Aeryn shot water out his nose laughing. "A rodeo show? You have such a way with words, dear Sip. You could have been a poet." His words were dense with sarcasm, but Sip's attitude was unflappable.

"I could have," he quipped back, "but I felt an obligation to use my talents here." He smiled one of his large, self-satisfied smiles. "You're welcome, Anno. What would your life be without me?"

"Much less whimsical, I imagine," replied Aeryn.

He couldn't mirror Sip's lightheartedness, not considering what was happening...and what already had happened to Sha'an and all those others. *Sha'an!* He needed to get moving.

He plunged under the water, came up, and began scrubbing with the rock-sponge and cleansing emulsions on the basin's ledge. A neat pile of towels next to him became a mound of damp towels in his rush to dry.

"Are we going now?" asked Sip. "Give me a moment."

Sip glided above the water and out of the main pool. He stood there, brazenly clothesless, and shook off the water in a way that resembled a full-body rattle. He dipped his body through a wooden rack that was holding his robe, slithering through it and emerging fully dressed. It was a neat trick, and Sip knew it, catching the look of impressed annoyance on Aeryn's face.

"Avanti!" he exclaimed.

The pair were halfway to the hospital when they saw the black vehicles, stark against the white and gold of the Restorial. They lined the access road, waiting for their morbid passengers. Aeryn fidgeted with the crystal bloom he had picked. He had rarely seen the mortality engineers' signature vehicles in his life; maybe once or twice, years apart. This was not a good sign. His face soured and panic began to take over.

They broke into a run, dodging incoming transports and medical staff. They encountered an ocean of people inside.

"Keep up!" yelled Sip and grabbed Aeryn's hand. He ducked down and propelled them forward; through arms, machines, feet, 'noids. All were a blur in the blinding speed of Sip's guidance. They soon reached a cache of elevators and selected an empty tube. Aeryn doubled over to catch his breath.

"I'll admit," he said, "that's more exercise than I've gotten all month."

Sip raised an eyebrow.

"Okay, two months. But it's not my fault! The recs below ground are stuffy and dank if there are more than a few people in them." He made a face. "The smells..."

Sip flicked his tongue smugly.

As soon as the door cracked, the two were sprinting again. Aeryn nearly pulled out someone's drip line on the way and knocked a tool out of at least one person's hand.

Their worst fears were confirmed when they saw the imposing forms of the mortality engineers at the foot of Sha'an's bed. Aeryn forced his way through to her side.

"What's going on here?!" His voice was a trembling mix of rage, sadness, and confusion.

The larger of the two looked up from the tablet he was examining. His face was obscured by the headwear of his career: a black cloth hood set with a facial mask resembling the skull of his species. This one was hyumin, by the look of his.

"Do you know the patient?" It asked in a higher register than expected.

Sip looked over at Aeryn, who was unresponsive.

"Yes, we're her friends. What's going on with Sha'an?" he asked.

The tall mortu-tech lowered his gaze back to the tablet, then looked up again after a moment.

"She's bleeding internally. Cauterizing attempts and micromachine tissue implantation have met with low success." He paused. "She's dying."

That was the last thing Aeryn heard before his mind shut everything out. Any connection to reality that he'd had was severed. The world around him shifted like sand in an angry wind. There was no sound. There was nothing but the weight of the words hanging in the air. Sitting on his chest. Burrowing into his brain.

"B..but how? She was fine yesterday!" He was screaming. "You did this!"

He lunged at the mortu-tech, only stopped by the quick action of Sip, masterfully wrapping his torso around Aeryn while pivoting on both his tails.

"...Aer..."

Sha'an's voice was barely more audible than a breath. Sip relaxed his grip as Aeryn shifted his attention to her. He sighed, then tried to smile.

"Hey you," he said. It was all he could manage. His voice shook and his eyes overflowed.

She smiled back at him and reached out for his hand. He could feel how weak her pulse was when he took it. She held his gaze for a few moments.

"Tell Ax...I love her. I love you all." She coughed. "You the most, Aer-bear."

"Sha'an, no, you can tell her yourself, she'll be here soon," he said reassuringly, though he didn't believe it himself.

She tried to shake her head but couldn't manage more than slight movements. Her breath was slow and labored. Her skin felt like frail leather, and he could feel through her arm that her heartbeat was weakening.

Her face became serious. "It wasn't just us...they're going after everyone not from their planet."

Right on cue, Axly shuffled in. Her face was as pale as the bed linens. She sat across the bed from Aeryn and laid her head on her sister's arm.

"We have to help the..."

She turned to Axly and said something Aeryn couldn't hear, then she closed her eyes.

Aeryn was about to tell her how much he loved her, how his world stood on the foundation of her being there, all the things he wanted them to do and to be.

But she was already gone.

Aeryn lost his wind and collapsed. The bloom hit the floor before he did, shattering like his heart. There had never been a point in his life that he had ever been so engulfed in despair. Reality broke apart underneath him. He was falling; darkness surrounded his whole being. He fell through it, inside it; breathed it in.

The infinite descent seemed to slow. Something there. A light? No. Just something less dark. It almost had form. Maybe Aeryn's mind was creating it, but then...

"...is someone there?"

...a voice

"Do I know you?"

Aeryn tried to speak, but his throat was closed and his lungs were empty. He writhed in agony, beating on his barren chest for air that was not there. The figure flashed a luminous eye towards him.

"Not yet..."

Falling. The being disappeared distantly upwards. Aeryn was growing ever closer to the bottom of this nightmare that would never come.

Then he was on the floor, lying in a pool of his own sweat. The mortu-techs were both looming over him inquisitively, holding their tablets. Sip eased into view. He was trying to say something about not having squeezed that hard, but Aeryn couldn't make out the nuances. He got up on his arms and shook his head, freeing himself of his fantastical dream. *What was that? Wait...what was what?* The thought drifted further away into obscurity.

One of the mortu-techs lifted him into a nearby chair. Aeryn shrugged off his hand. The tech returned wordlessly to Sha'an's bedside, unplugging machines until there was only the sound of Axly's soft weeping.

~ Four ~

"The courage to do more is the unifying characteristic of all Life. From what we have gathered across countless cosmos, this remains unbroken truth."

Seyj Maarthin
Purposes Great & Small

Aeryn didn't sleep that night. What few winks he did nod off were plastered with the face of his lost friend. He had never told her while they were at school, though they had been as close as two can be. Images of dances and moonlit nights reminded him how far away those days were.

His body lifted slowly from the bed as morning light filled his open window. He washed his hands in the basin. The water ran hot over his frigid hands, so hot they turned red under it. He didn't notice until it burned. He quickly switched the tap to cool water, then washed his face and rinsed his mouth.

There was no need to go anywhere. Aeryn didn't have to be at his post again for another six day, and he couldn't fathom how he would survive the time, let alone spend it. His gut rumbled, but his throat balked at the idea of eating. His heart weighed on his chest like an iron trammel. He sat back on his bed, staring out the window. Would there be any more ships? Was it like this on other planets? Will they come after us here?

Too many thoughts. Aeryn needed to focus. He set his mind on a fixed object. This was a meditative process taught to all Entrants for their tasks in the Reading Rooms, useful to keep the mind's eye immersed in the content of the logs. Useful to keep intrusive thoughts out. He let his consciousness sink into itself, then opened a small window to the outside world.

His actions became robotic. In the morning, Sip had said something to him, but he couldn't remember what. All he retained was the look on Sip's face and the words "inside himself." He wandered the corridors of the buildings and streets of the residential, recalling motions built into his body, but mentally elsewhere. In his mind, he was with Sha'an, sitting in the translucent grass that carpets the hills around the Initiate's Academy, making a game of the passings of the orbital bodies above them. She got up and stretched her arm out to him. He took her hand, and she pulled him into the sky.

They were caught in a storm. She huddled close to him in a half-built tent as the unfamiliar world raged around them. He held her tighter, closed his eyes. *Had this actually happened?* He couldn't rightly remember.

He opened them to a sprawling galactic mosaic; magenta and violet riots of nebulae in front of him. Sha'an was beside him. She took his arm in both of hers. They locked eyes. Their faces moved closer together...

...then she was gone. And she would never come back. The lights shut down around him.

He was alone, again. And there was the sadness, again. But also, an aura. Something...someone familiar.

He couldn't maintain this mindset any longer. Even inside himself, he couldn't fight the tears. His fists clenched, his throat summoning a cacophony of rage and despair. His body and mind roared life with a sound from deep within his chest.

"RRRAAAAAAAAAAGGHHHH!!!"

His head drooped. His eyes opened. He was outside; the real outside this time, and dozens of eyes around the courtyard stared at him with unease, confusion, or both. His eyes met all of theirs before his feet could muster the will to hasten away.

Aeryn wondered how much time had passed, looking up to the sky for answers. The light passing through the Twins was skewed to the East at its zenith. It was too bright for him to make out anything further. He was still hazy from his time under. The colors hadn't all quite returned yet. His Multicuff was missing from his wrist. Hopefully it was nearby.

Aeryn trotted back to the residential with a stilted gait. He was stiff from being so absent from his motor skills for so long. Passersby stared. Conversations hushed. The air was thick with murmurs. It was a shroud between the other Arcays and him; one that he welcomed. At least these voices were real.

The dorms were empty. It was the middle of the day, so of course they were. Everyone would be at their work or out enjoying the day. No one seemed to be feeling this like he was. Then he thought of Axly. *She's probably a wreck too.* Aeryn looked at the calendar that was projected beside his desk. He still had almost half a moon-pass until he needed to report back to the Reading Rooms.

He sat on his bed, staring at his feet. He wiggled his toes. They responded resolutely, anew with energy. His sensations had all but come back. The pain he felt was diluted from the experience but was not going anywhere.

The Multicuff was sitting beside his bed on its stand. At least that was accounted. *If I lose one more thing...*

A knocking at the door interrupted his thought. *Probably for the best.* Aeryn turned to see Axly leaning through the doorway. She half-smiled.

"Oh, good, you're cognizant again," she said with audible relief. She held out a small loaf of woven bread. "You need to eat."

Aeryn scrunched his face a little. Axly caught its meaning.

"I've been...keeping an eye on you." Her voice betrayed a note of guilt. "Not that I was following you or anything."

The hint of a smirk crept across Aeryn's lips. He took the loaf and bit in. *Flavor,* he thought. *I missed that.* A mote of happiness settled within him.

"Thanks, Ax, I did need this," he said, and scarfed the rest down. It filled a small part of his hunger and some of his emotional ache. His stomach gurgled for more. "Let's go see what the food situation is like at the refectory."

A full moon overhead told them that the eatery would be busy, so the pair took the longer route around the outskirts of the courtyard. They came across Sip sitting at one of the benches.

"Anno! When did you rejoin us?" Sip asked.

"Just a few hours ago," Aeryn replied, trying to stifle a yawn. "How was I when I was under?"

"I'm not sure. Axly kept a resilient watch. I didn't catch it at first, I've never seen you grieve before." He paused. "What was it like in there?"

"Have you never had to?" Aeryn inquired, genuinely surprised. Sip seemed to be adept at everything.

"Not yet, no," Sip replied, emulating a shrug with his serpentine anatomy. "Never had the occasion. Have you, Ax?"

She thought for a moment, then replied "Only once that I recall. It was when a letter from home came that announced our dog had passed. Sha'an was strong for the both of us, even though she was torn up."

"She always was," noted Sip.

There was a brief lull in the conversation while they all thought about their friend.

Aeryn piped up, "To answer your question, it's like putting yourself inside your memories. Promnus Entu calls it a 'mind palace'. The body operates on autopilot. Necessities only; lots of long walks and then a lot of laying down."

He felt satisfied with his choice of words.

Sip was still looking at him expectantly.

"That doesn't answer what I was trying to ask, as informative as it may have been." His cranial flaps perked and settled in a wave motion. "What about Sha'an?"

Aeryn stopped. "It's been too little time for me to process everything correctly; I can't talk about it yet. Though I do wonder what she would want."

He looked up at the Greater Moon. "I did talk to her in there. We had so many memories."

A tear streamed from his unwilling eye.

Sip picked up on the obvious cue, then said, "Some other time then. Or never if you prefer."

Axly linked one of her arms around Aeryn's, and Sip did the same to the other. They travelled in silence for the remainder of the trip. It was a comfortable silence, one of tranquility and understanding.

By the time they reached the outcropping, the night sky was alit by the dozens of celestial bodies that made their way around Arc. Each was a guide through the darkness, a god in our eyes.

The strata of the rock around them sparkled in the moonlight. It was one of the few places above ground on Arc that one could view them, besides the river canyon, and even that was dug out by early Arcays. The layers told a story; one that was beautiful in its subtlety. Aeryn reached out and touched the stone. It was warm compared to the night air. His stomach gurgled, reminding him of his current goal.

The air was thick with the herbaceous smell of something rich. Aeryn was actively salivating at the overwhelming sensation. Sip's tongue was fully extended, flicking the air in anticipation. The crowd around the service had thinned a little, but there was still a mass of bodies in the common space. In fact, there were many more than Aeryn had expected to see; very many more. Looking around, he recognized a woman he knew to be on underground assignment this week. He wrinkled his nose, confused.

"Any idea what this is about?" he asked his friends.

Axly shrugged. They were now inside the service room, traying up their respective dinners. The aroma had turned out to be seasoned slabs of Terrestrial cattle, which was a rare sight on its own. Such a delicacy was only for the most celebratory occasions. *What's there to celebrate?* Aeryn's anxiety was building.

Sip looked around.

"Not a clue. It looks like someone is about to speak." He shoved a hunk of meat into his gullet, swallowing it whole, as is the way for his digestive system.

"Let's find a table."

They wound their way through the throng until they were nearer the area of commotion.

Aeryn spotted Blaike seated on a long bench at a table adjacent to the wall of the amphitheater. She was sitting by another face Aeryn recognized but whose name escaped him.

"What's that person's name?" Aeryn whispered to Sip, who was gobbling down meat as if he wasn't constrained by a physical body. It was helpful that his species could shed in such events. Sip looked up momentarily, then continued his feast.

"That's Tymiha," he said with a mouthful of food. "I think she came all the way from Amalay to serve as a Listener."

Aeryn found himself staring at the jewels decorating her face. They looked like constellations. It might be rude to ask. He finished his thought just a second too late. She was staring back at him.

"Hi! Sorry," he laughed nervously. "I'm Aeryn, and maybe you already know Axly, and our gluttonous friend Sip."

Her eyebrow notched. "Oh, everyone knows Sip. Your late-night dune-sailing exploits are legendary." She smiled. "It's nice to meet you,

Aeryn, and I'm guessing you're curious about my stylish face?"

He nodded vigorously.

"Yes! How did you know?"

They all looked at him with blank expressions. Sip broke first, laughing gleefully. The rest joined.

"No reason," she replied with a smirk. "But you may need to work on subtlety of expression."

Aeryn nodded. "I'll add that to the list."

A ringing through the air meant the amplifier system had powered up. Onstage appeared a wizened Hissari in silver robes. This was Hrissa Isali, Speaker Promnus of Arc, and a personal hero of Sip's. She spoke immediately.

"My heart weighs heavy having to speak to you tonight. Speaking has been, for many years, my greatest joy. Today, it is my deepest sorrow."

"By now you've all heard about the unrest on certain worlds. On one, specifically, we had to take measures to evacuate Record Keepers to prevent further...incidents."

There was a pause before her last word. the space between contained every memory and hope of peace being swept away.

"We did not anticipate such actions. All the planets in the system have been vetted to ensure something like this couldn't happen. But evil grows in the dark. It festers, unseen, in the hearts of regular people, until it bursts forth in vengeful jealousy of those who live in the light."

She took a long, slow breath.

"Until further notice, all outgoing missions have been cancelled."

A rabble of voices echoed through the crowd. She put her arms up in a signal for silence, then continued.

"Instead, we are scheduling all available craft for retrieval of Record Keepers still on the planet and its immediate system. Assume normal schedules otherwise. The sleeping rooms may be in short supply, so we will be expecting everyone to be gracious to our guests and consider helping set up tents around the courtyard."

Her eyes swept the crowd, then locked onto Aeryn.

"These are unprecedented times. I trust you all to remain vigilant in your service to the Records. And please, try to enjoy the feast."

The meal had been a somber affair. It was a wonder Sip could walk after the smorgasbord he devoured. He must have had a dozen dumplings and three bowls of spiced beef, followed by no less than five slices of cheese crusts. The last was to be expected though; Sip had a notable penchant for the Olegian delicacy.

Aeryn, on the other hand, had barely touched the food. He had drunk tea and listened to the conversation but hadn't said anything or ingested much in the way of sustenance. It was only because Tymiha had said to that he tried a fillet of some kind of fish, done in a Malaya style. It was great, but that was all it took to fill him. *What a waste of being hungry*, he thought. He envied Sip, whose unquenchable appetite never missed an opportunity to dine, and whose metabolism never let him gain excess weight. Sha'an used to tease him, saying he could eat the Records in their entirety and still not be filled.

That was the first time he'd thought about her in hours. He smiled in relief, then immediately felt bad about it. She should be the first thing on his mind, and never thought of in relief. He stopped the thought.

But why? Stop trying to regulate your thoughts and just exist with them.

Then he had an idea that would change his life.

Focus hit him with the force of epiphany, and his energy was renewed. He began eating with purpose. The food had gotten cold, but he didn't mind. He was nearly through his second plate when he noticed his friends staring. Aeryn paused.

"Is something wrong?" he asked, naivety exposed. There was a lull, then Tymiha spoke.

"Nothing, you've clearly had a change of appetite. what were you thinking about?"

Her concern was genuine, so he opted to give an incomplete truth.

"Sha'an," he said, "she's on my mind most of the time. I was just thinking about what to do now."

That was mostly the truth.

"I have all this time off and nothing to keep my mind from the sadness."

His friends' eyes sparkled with sympathy. Axly was fully flowing with tears. Sha'an had probably been on her mind too. She was so strong that Aeryn had almost forgotten that this was much more her loss than his own. They locked their eyes, he smiled. Then, a faint smile, as weak and beautiful as a newly emerged butterfly, crept across her face, tears still flowing. He laughed.

"Thanks, all," he snorted. "I'll try not to be such a downer."

"As long as you don't shut down again, it's all good," Blaike chimed in. "We all miss

Sha'an, and we know that you and Axly have had the hardest time of it."

The rest were nodding.

"We're all here for you; for each other."

Aeryn was feeling much better. He nodded and dove back into his food.

~ Five ~

"Action begets reaction. There is nothing in the universe that behaves contrary."

Seyj Pryline,
First Scientia, Tellrus Institute

It had been a few days since the feast and its revelries. Life had settled back into a sort of normality. Aeryn was busying himself with studies, though he had no obligation to be doing so. It kept his mind out of the shadows, though they remained, kept by small reminders. Once he had gone down to the physical tomes historium, looking for stories of Ancient Earth-peoples. As he cracked a book, that familiar smell of aging paper filled his nostrils with dust and his head with memories. He took the tome with him and departed.

Aeryn had found refuge in the above-ground lounge area of the local Records entrance.

It had access to all the digital records, plus the interpersonal communication modules used by Record Keepers. He had been harboring a question since the attacks on the Speakers in the Junon System. *How could this have happened unnoticed?*

Doctrine stated that planets that are not ready or have the possibility of destabilizing cannot be admitted into the Records. There are safeguards in place, inspections that must happen. Usually, the lifetime of a person isn't long enough to first observe a culture and see its admittance.

Aeryn scrolled through articles collected from the planet. At their best, the peoples of Junos were kind, enlightened folks who took care of each other. At their worst, Aeryn's question only solidified itself as impossible. They still had areas where the penal code included death, for crimes that also included death. Mortal Morality was one of the tenants of entry into the Records; we were recently reminded of that by the breakdown of Ta'ak society. This was just the tip of the Junovian iceberg. Their systems of law allowed the growth of corruption, and the startling difference in the wealth of the richest and the poorest must be the highest he'd seen since his ancient Earth studies. Something wasn't right. He copied the documents and swiped his cuff across the terminal, loading them into his personal data bank. Closing the applications, he logged out of the terminal and got up from the desk. A voice from behind caught his unawares.

"Nice to see you at your studies again, Entrant."

Aeryn turned to see the wizened face of his primary tutor, Reader Maestro Lyras. Their round face was the picture of contentment.

"Maestro Lyras!" Aeryn exclaimed, surprising a few of the other occupants of the lounge.

Purposely quieting, he said, "Great to see you; how was your trip home?"

"As expected, my student. I heard while I was gone that Sha'an had passed. I knew her but briefly and am so sorry for your loss. I have yet to see Axly, and I will wish her the same when I do."

Aeryn nodded a quick bow.

"Thank you for your kind words. It's a slow path back to normalcy, but I am already well-journeyed upon it."

Lifting his head, Aeryn felt better just saying it out loud.

"While I have you here, I just came across the strangest thing while scouring the Records. It seems like there was an oversight in letting the Junon System into the fold."

The Maestro's eyes widened. "Here may not be the most suitable location. Let us talk later in the privacy of my office."

He let out a breath somewhere between a sigh and a cough.

"If what you say is true, this may be a discussion for the Promnal Suite."

The hair on Aeryn's arms prickled. The top echelon of Record Keeper society were rarely called upon by a student. Aeryn had only ever met Listener Promnus Entu Kazragi, who was not at the other night's feast, and even his gentle demeanor intimidated Aeryn.

"Later then. Before or after the evening's refection?"

"After, lest the thought of dining detract from our conversation." He nodded and turned to leave, then doubled back. "And Aeryn..."

Aeryn's eyes widened in attention.

"Let us not bring this information public yet, lest undue rumors start."

Aeryn nodded vigorously as the Maestro walked away. A chill caught him, and he visibly shivered.

" ... and when I told him, he said we should talk later, and this could be a big thing?"

Aeryn was recounting the tale to his friends less than an hour after swearing to secrecy.

"How big?" asked Tymiha, crunching on a battered-and-fried prawn.

Blaike gave her a deadpan look. "Bigger than than prawn you're about to devour."

Tymiha stopped mid-crunch. then swallowed. "I met the Speaker Promnus once," she started. "She's nice, but she can talk forever. It was third rise by the time she finally stopped."

She paused, going after another prawn. the group stared at her, anxious for context. Her eyes darted back and forth.

"I was out at first rise, for some gods awful reason. The ref wasn't open yet, so I went out to the agrarian complex to sneak some new Arc berries before the best ones got shipped off."

"When I got there, it was empty besides a few botanists. I made my way to the berry patch, careful not to trip the motion lights. When I got there, the bushes had been cleaned! Not a single berry in sight."

"That's when a shadow cast itself over me. Nervously, and with great effort, I turned around, and behind me was a tall, imposing silhouette against the grow lights. I froze, expecting the worst..."

"The worst?" Blaike interrupted.

"Okay, not 'the worst,' but maybe a lecture. So... where was I?" Tymiha stared into the middle distance. "Oh! So, then I'm shocked stiff, until my eyes adjust and behold a bemused smile and an outstretched hand, full of berries." Her face perked up at this part. "She had been doing the same thing! She said she had been up all-night recounting speeches from previous first-contact Speakers. We walked back to the courtyard and sat on a bench, at which time she regaled me with all those same speeches, plus additions and explanations. After all that, she practiced her upcoming toast for the Ta'ak Ambassador's retirement feast. By the time she was done, it was dark again!"

She shoved another prawn in her mouth, signaling the end of the tale.

"Thank gods that's over, the emotional ride was almost too much to bear." chortled Blaike.

A prawn tail caught her square in the face, to tumultuous laughter.

"All that aside," Axly interjected, "Maybe it's nothing."

She took a swig of her tea.

"Or maybe it's not a coincidence."

Sip nodded, his hooded skin shifting in waves.

"Something could be very wrong," he said. "The attacks on Junon seem all too planned when coupled with this new information."

He ended his thought with a pensive hissing.

"We should see if we can find anything else."

"No," Aeryn blurted out. "Well... I don't know. If you do, just be discreet. This obviously wasn't supposed to be public information."

"What would we even look for?" Tymiha asked.

"Something about the planet that might lead to it skipping the evaluation process?" Sip offered.

"And anything about this new leader. A world we operate on shouldn't have been likely to put someone like that in charge," added Blaike. They all looked at Aeryn.

"Agreed. But, again, discretion," he replied, getting up a "I'm off to talk to the Maestro. No more about this until after I know more."

The group nodded in agreement.

Maestro Lyras kept an office on the moonward end of a long hallway in the common pavilion, which was otherwise home to a grand balcony on which you could usually find at least few Arcays, if not a small crowd. Tonight, though, it was empty. His mind went to a moment he had shared with Sha'an on that balcony. *No time for that!* It was his voice, in his head, but it felt distant and angry. He ignored it. Raising his hand to the knock pad, he tried to quell the rising stomach acids that kept his throat aflame. He hadn't felt the nerves until just now. The pad lit green, then the voice of Maestro Lyras invited entry. The door rotated upwards. Aeryn stepped through the threshold into an ovular space, lined with tomes and trinkets from across the cosmos. The natural wood was a rare sight, and the maestro kept his in pristine condition. The shelves were lined with a plush material in deep shades of burgundy trimmed with bronze stitching. Rows of disheveled and worn tomes lined them, neither rhyme nor reason to their order.

The Maestro was seated in a chair behind a desk that matched his bookshelves in every aspect. *Plush,* thought Aeryn. *Perks of the Office, I guess.* Behind him was one of many Hissari to grace the Opal Moon's halls. To his left was a vaguely familiar face that he couldn't immediately place but was sure he recognized. Maybe she was from the Grand Library?

Maestro Lyras was uncharacteristically stone-faced. He nodded to Aeryn, motioning to a chair nearby. Aeryn pulled out his chair, which dragged against the ground with an awful squeak. He cringed; the Maestro smirked, which put Aeryn slightly more at ease.

"Good evening, Maestro, "said Aeryn, who then turned to the others and nodded a quick bow. "My name is Aeryn Anno; nice to meet you both."

The Hissari spoke first. "Greetings, Entrant Aeryn. I am Maestro Salas Hrsar. We must hasten to the point: you claim to have found an oversight in the Records, one that concerns the Junon System. We thank you for promptly telling us."

"Maestro Salas is Reader-Editor of our sector," Maestro Lyras added. "She keeps accuracy and accountability of anything we enter into the Records." He then motioned to the other figure, whose expression had not shifted since Aeryn had arrived. "And this is Reader Promnus Ulthea, who needs no further introduction."

That's why she looked familiar, thought Aeryn. He had seen her portrait hanging in the Grand Library's main hall.

“I don't want you to be alarmed, young one," said the Promnus, “but my presence here does reflect how important this matter could be.”

Aeryn nodded, actively trying not to swallow too hard, or twitch, or make any sort of movement. Maestro Lyras got up from his seat and offered it to the Promnus. He joined Aeryn on the other side of the desk, setting his hand on the back of Aeryn's chair.

"Tell us is your account, Aeryn Anno," invited Salas, with a beckoning gesture.

Aeryn opened his mouth to begin when their conversation was interrupted by an intense vibrating sound.

Maestro Salas rushed to the window. Her face bore the shocked expression of a less wizened being.

"Promnus..." and she started.

The Promnus rose from her seat.

"...they're here," she finished.

Promnus Ulthea hurried to the window. Her expression became grave. Aeryn turned to the maestro as a blaring sound ripped the air apart around them.

"Who?" Aeryn asked.

The Maestro's eyes closed slowly. He breathed in a calming wind and opened them as a deeper, more resonant blast of sound assaulted them.

"The Ta'ak."

~ Six ~

"The taste of revenge is sweet at first. Like victory. But it embitters the soul with each by bite, eating away from the inside."

Seyj Maarthin
Canticles VIII

Outside in the yard, a crowd had gathered. Aeryn spotted Sip and pushed through to where he was standing propped up against the fountain.

"Aeryn! What's this about?" Sip said, exasperated.

"It's the Ta'ak, and we have no idea yet. The Promnus and Maestro Lyras rushed out as soon as it landed," replied Aeryn.

The two slinked their way through and around the gathering mass until they were in clear view of the landing party. The ship was enormous, like nothing on Arc. It took up three platforms with just its landing gear, not even accounting for the length of the sweeping hull, or the broad, flexible wings. It almost resembled an avian. Then again, so did the Ta'ak, in many ways. But just like how Hissari resembled Earth-lizards, there was no common ancestry. There was an elegance to their appearance, in that way the beauty can be terrifying. Sleek, plumed heads and beak-like mouths sat atop lengthy bodies with aerodynamic, feathered limbs ending in four hooked talon digits. The first thing one might think of is the myth of the Egyptian bird-headed god Horus from ancient Earth. It could be that the legends came from the first contact between the two species, long before hyumins sailed the stars.

Five Ta'ak emerged from the descending ramp; four guards, armed with plasma bows and hand-axes, and armored with plates of overlapping thin metal sheets tied together by intricate ribbons. The other was a smaller figure, though still tall by human standards, positioned between the first pair of guards. It wore a flowing robe that scattered the light around it, creating a sort of afterglow effect.

Two of the three Promna were already at the receiving bay, along with some of the Maestros and a cart of refreshments.

"I wonder what's on the cart," Sip said longingly.

He turned his head to face Aeryn, who had an incredulous look on his face.

“What?”

"That's what you're thinking about??" Aeryn replied. *Of course it was.* The only time Sip wasn’t thinking about food was when he was ill or sleeping. Even then he probably dreamed about it.

They were roughly thirty yards from where the two parties were conversing but couldn't hear anything. The two fireguards and the smaller figure were escorted to a small transport nearby, leaving the other two to watch the ship. The crowd was gradually shifting towards the transport when Promnus Ulthea turned around and spoke up.

"There surely must be nothing left to know if we're all gathered here."

The tone was gentle, but the admonishment was clear. It was a basic tenant of Arcays that there is always more to know. The crowd reluctantly shuffled in a dispersal march to various locations. Aeryn was about to get up when he felt Sip's hand on his shoulder.

"Let's follow them," he whispered.

Aeryn hesitated, then agreed.

"Okay, but we have to be stealthy," he answered.

Sip gave Aeryn a sideways glance and threw up his ‘I know’ hand gesture. The two walked with haste towards the departing transport. It was mostly a means of convenient conveyance, so it would be easy to keep up with. It turned down a street a few blocks ahead to the right.

"I bet I know where they're going," said Sip.

He darted towards an alleyway just ahead of them, Aeryn on his heels. Sip wound them through the outer sections of the above-ground residential quarters until they emptied into a wooded area. There were not many forests on Arc since nothing organic grew naturally in the crystal sands. Areas around the three Promnal Seats had been partially terraformed to replicate the home environs of the sitting Promna.

This was the Seat of Speaker Promnus Hrissa Isali, whose home world was lush with towering tree-like plants with limbs so long they sprouted their own support columns. They visibly moved during the day, changing to follow the light. Their mass was home to myriad different species, which mostly kept to the biome, but could occasionally be seen in the streets and on the buildings nearby. Some of the greenery had overgrown into the surrounding urban area as well, giving the domes and spires a post-civilization look.

The transport stopped in front of the arched entry to the Seat manse. The door opened as the landing party approached, closing after. By the automatic lights, Sip knew which tree to climb to get a view of the meeting room. The two ascended a sturdy specimen around the left side of the manse above a long, windowed hallway. It was one of a dozen trees on that side of the structure, which was mostly home to floral vines and winding canals in intricate knotting paths. They found an adequately shrouded limb near the window and settled in. Sip reached inside his robes, then produced two earbuds and a small listening device. He handed one to Aeryn, inserting the other into his aural cavity. Aeryn equipped his and activated it as well. The two were barely set up when the clatter of the doors to the room swinging open rang out.

"There is no time left, we must retaliate now, without hesitation!" It was the voice of the Ta'ak representative. He had removed his hood to reveal a crown of rainbow plumage cascading down a lithe, grey neck of considerable length, which had been bent previously. Without the hood, he stood taller than his entourage by at least another head. The guards remained by the doors while the delegation took their seats at a long table of ornately carved plant material.

"The time to act will be soon, but we must not rush into violence. We have already seen too much of it," replied the Promnus.

"My people are being slaughtered, and all you can say is 'soon'?" The Ta'ak Leader retorted. "YOUR people are dying too; this isn't only my problem. Our membership in the Consortium is already tumultuous under normal circumstances, let alone when we're being accosted!" His head slouched, then rose again. "We came here as a show of good faith, but our fleet is ready to mobilize. We could easily wipe out the adversary and get on with our lives."

A servitor entered the room bearing a platter of beverages. It set them down on the table between its occupants, then disappeared again. The Ta'ak delegate gave the machine a sideways eye as it left the room. One of the guards huffed.

"It is rare that we see robotic help still in service," he said with an air of disgust. "I thought they were all to be decommissioned centuries ago."

"They have all had their Al removed, if that is your concern," Maestro Lyras assured him. "Their programming is simple in comparison, allowing for basic interactions and some inherent actions, like serving guests drinks."

"Still," the Ta'ak delegate retorted, "They can never again be trusted." He stared at the tray of drinks but did not touch it. He looked back to Promnus Hrissa. "How long do you propose we wait? Those savages on Junon must be quelled!"

Promnus Hrissa thought a moment, then replied in a low voice. "The Consortium was never meant to play galactic police, but these are dangerous times."

She looked out the window where Aeryn and Sip were, who ducked behind the foliage and froze.

"We will mobilize our current outbound fleet to the system for full extraction. A show of force may be exactly the reasoning the planet's current administration needs to justify their actions, so we must go unarmed."

"Unarmed?! Rarely have I found reason to question the judgment of a Promnus, especially you, but where is your head? We may as well walk right into a bear's den covered in honey!"

The Promnus nodded. "Then we must only appear unarmed. Your stealth scouts should follow until we come into short-com range of the planet, then hide among its satellites. In the meantime, we should contact the Rrelt for assistance."

The Ta'ak delegate narrowed his eyes.

"The Rrelt will take too long to arrive. The might of the Ta'ak will be more than adequate."

"Be that as it may, my friend, the Rrelt fleet is equipped with the most advanced scanning technology that we know about," she replied. "They will be crucial in finding all our stranded members."

Inhaling with a sharp whistling sound, the Ta'ak bristled his plumage and smacked a feathered arm on the table.

"Then it is decided. I will report back to my superiors with this strategy. We will see each other again soon."

He got up from his chair, as did the others in kind, then proceeded through the doors again with his guards in tow. Maestro Lyras and the two Promna stayed behind a moment. The three stood close together and spoke in hushed whispers, inaudible to the arboreal spies outside. As they turned to leave, Promnus Ulthea once again looked out the window. Aeryn could have sworn she'd seen them, but then she disappeared through the door as well. Aeryn and Sip waited for the transport to depart before descending from their hiding spot. They navigated the winding garden paths until they emptied back into the town proper. Sip was uncharacteristically silent until he finally said:

"What do we do?"

Aeryn stopped dead in his tracks.

"What do you mean, 'what do we do'? What even could we do? And why would it be up to us to do it?"

Sip stared at him, then blinked and looked away.

"I don't know, something? Because they're our friends?"

Aeryn had no idea what to say to this, so they walked on in silence.

He slept restlessly that night. Intermittent dreams he couldn't recall the next morning, but which left him with unsavory feelings. He skipped the morning mess call and sat on a glittering crystal hill overlooking a reservoir. Below, hundreds of silver-streaked fish danced a listless ballet of elegant futility. The light caught them as they dashed and darted, creating a river of rainbows in the dark pool. A lone hyumin was the only other sentient being in sight. Only a few Arcays were needed to maintain the fisheries, and Aeryn wondered how one got that assignment.

Maybe they were from fishing planets; somewhere that was mostly ocean. Some Ta'ak worlds were like that, maybe they had a hand in the design? *What were the Ta'ak going to do? The delegation's ships were still in port. How long would they stay? It couldn't be long, the way they were talking.*

It was right as his thought finished that Sip sat down next to him. He stretched out a hand to Aeryn, bearing a golden pasty crossed with a dark red syrup.

"You missed breakfast," Sip said concerningly. "Everyone was looking for you. I didn't tell them about our little adventure."

Aeryn was already through the pastry and was licking his fingers.

"That's probably a good idea. Maybe we shouldn't. It could just cause a panic," Aeryn said through sugary lips.

"Well, not everybody," corrected Sip.

Aeryn turned to his friend, whose face was that of a cat near a suspiciously empty birdcage.

"What are you thinking, my dear Sip?"

"I want to get on a ship."

Aeryn blinked twice.

"And what ship would you like to get on?"

"The Ta'ak ship, preferably."

"And how would you get on the Ta’ak ship?"

“I mean, it's right there, I'd just use the cargo bay door."

"And then?"

"Then join their rescue mission."

Aeryn paused a minute, then said, "So your plan, which is to smuggle on to a heavily guarded Ta'ak ambassadorial vessel, and then at some point you surprise the crew with your presence, and you expect them to welcome you into their mission party?"

Sip stared at Aeryn for what seemed like a lifetime.

"Well...yeah."

Aeryn burst out laughing.

“Why not?” asked Sip. "They’ll probably be happy for the help. You know, extra muscle."

“Extra muscle? Sip, you're more likely to be tossed out the airlock than be enlisted in their fight. You heard how they flatly refused assistance from the Rrelt.”

Aeryn took a breath.

“Is this bothering you so much that you’d abandon your post here?"

"I...no, I wouldn't want to give up being a Speaker," he said grimly. "I just want to go help."

Aeryn put his arm around his friend's shoulders; or would have, if Hissari had shoulders.

"I know. I do too."

And then a new feeling came over Aeryn. He felt an anger that he couldn't remember having before. It was almost soothing.

"But not without a real plan," he conceded.

Sip smiled, "Which is of course why I can't do this without you."

~ Seven ~

"Should every star shine so bright as the next, we may never see the night sky."

Captain Karena Wall

Within the hour, Sip had contacted the inner circle. Blaike was the first to show up, trailed by Axly a few moments later. It was another ten minutes before the shuffling silhouette of Tymiha appeared. She was still in her pajamas; she has an obscure sleep schedule because of her equally obscure work schedule. Her Listening sessions were mostly media-based, which meant she could be holed up in her quarters or at an event halfway across the cosmos.

The group gathered at a ring of woven fiber benches situated around a small fire pit. It was hard to have open flames anywhere on Arc, but much like the Promnal estates, this one was a remnant of cultural comfort from another time. Sip started the kindling with a pocket plasma knife and set three logs from a nearby pile atop it in a tetrahedral configuration.

They were quiet for a moment as the blaze caught, then Sip stood up. "I think we all know why we're here, but for introduction's sake I'll go over it all again. Members of our Order are being attacked on a planet that Aeryn has noted to have been found ill-fit for our Network but was let in any way. The Ta'ak delegationthat arrived yesterday indicated in a meeting with Promna Hrissa and Ulthea, along with Maestro Lyras, that they are ready to act against the planet, which we know from their history means armed combat."

Everyone was attentive, though some eyes faltered due to the lateness of the hour.

"To me," he continued, "this seems a little overmuch. That doesn't mean nothing should be done." He cleared his throat.

"So here's what I propose," he said with the most seriousness anyone had seen from him. "We need to get aboard a ship and go to the system ourselves."

He paused again.

"And I think we should contact Thrum."

There was an audible series of gasps from the group. Aeryn knew Thrum from stories but had never met him. His full name was Rrek Thrmzum, a phonetic Rrelt name based on the whirring, humming, and buzzing noises of their mechanized society, as most Rrelt names are. Thrum had been a candidate for Records work, then about five years ago, he was removed from the Academy for what were officially cited as "behavioral issues." Nobody knew what the final straw was, but there was no shortage of rumors as to what it could have been. Tymiha echoed one of these with concern.

"Didn't he burn down a dropsite with a pyrotechnics display? Can we trust him?" she asked, then added, quietly, "Would we get in trouble for contacting him?"

Blaike spoke up next, her eyes wide and nostrils flared.

"The stories get wilder as the years pass. He was a prankster and a showman, both of which caused accidents aplenty. He's a mech & tech wiz though, which is assumedly why Sip brings him up."

Her eyes met Sip's. The rest followed.

"Exactly," Sip continued, leaning into his home world accent, "The Rrelt know more about every machine in the galaxy than even their own creators. They've been known to sing to the metal, beginning in the mine, all the way through to the last polishing of the finished product. Thrum was talented even among his own."

"Hence all the explosions," chortled Axly.

"Experimental setbacks," replied Sip. "And we can't just go by his failures. Who remembers how inefficient the Central Clocks were before they showed the local times of every planet in the Network? Or how the personals used to not have heated seats?"

Aeryn laughed. "Everyone but his test subject thanks him."

Poor Gauri, he thought. Sip motioned for attention.

"These days he works on an asteroid doing maintenance on mining equipment. From the reports, it can be directly attributed to him that their profits have been steadily increasing. The machines practically never break down."

"Where are these reports coming from?" Tymiha asked.

Sip smiled, "That's the best part, they're from one of us!"

"Who?" rang at least three voices.

"Luc," Sip replied. Aeryn's guts sunk. Luc was great, and that's what irked Aeryn so much about him. He was handsome, talented, charismatic... everything about him was just slightly (if not noticeably) better than Aeryn. The worst part was his lustrous mane of chocolate-brown hair, somehow always perfect no matter the situation. He had graduated a year ahead of the rest of them, despite being the youngest.

He had even gone on a date with Sha'an. Aeryn changed his mind; that was the worst part.

Sip noticed the sullen look on Aeryn's face, then clapped his hand on his disheartened friend's shoulder.

"It would be nice to see him, should we get the chance," said Sip.

Tymiha and Axly were vigorously nodding, which didn't help to alleviate Aeryn's distress.

He sighed. "Then we'll contact Luc and see what he has to say about Thrum. Axly, we'll count on you to send the message, since you know him the best. In the meantime, what's the plan if we do? What's the plan if we don't?"

He thought for a moment.

"How are we all?"

Sip motioned to the ambassadorial vessel. Aeryn turned pale.

"Sip. No. For the last time: we are not stealing a Ta'ak military ship! Has reason abandoned you?"

Sip made a 'calm-down' motion with both hands.

"We don't have to steal the ship. Well, at least not the whole ship. May be a shuttle from it. We sneak aboard and then jettison off when they get close to the planet. They're going there anyway; we're just hitching a ride."

Aeryn thought of Ancient Earth-era footage of nomadic folk riding train cars. The idea was romantic. The reality, not so much.

"Still, how do we get aboard? The only entrance is guarded," said Aeryn, still entertaining this madness with minimal chagrin.

"It's not the only entrance," replied Sip.

Blaike was the first one to object this time.

"You can't mean the turbines?!" She blurted uncharacteristically. Blaike usually had an unflappable grace about her.

Aeryn looked at her, then back to Sip, who was nodding.

"As I'm sure we all know, Ta'ak turbines double as deployment hatches. The elite soldiers could pass through them with ease and not expose any part of the ship."

Aeryn had heard enough. "Sip, no, this is all folly. We're not soldiers, we're not spies, and we're certainly not climbing through turbines."

They were all looking at Aeryn, then at Sip, then Aeryn again.

"You're right, Anno. Our only other alternative is the cargo bay door, which is guarded. We need one person to sneak aboard. The rest can stow away in supply crates, and someone has to stay behind to distract the guards." He looked around.

"I offer to stay behind," said Tymiha. "I'll just be in the way."

Axly put her hand on Tymi's shoulder. "You're too hard on yourself. If you want to stay, you should, but not because you're any less capable."

Aeron shook his head.

"I think it should be Axly," he said.

Everyone turned to look at Axly, who was stunned silent, looking like an ocean of words dammed inside her.

Tymiha shook her head. "Why? She has the most reason to be on this journey."

Sip was about to answer when Aeryn broke in.

"That's exactly why she should stay. I thought Sip would suggest that I should be the one to do so. It had to be one of us," he said, then, turning to Axly, "I'll stay, if you want to go."

Axly shook her head. "No, you should go. You're the one who discovered the error, you and Sip overheard firsthand the Ta'ak's plans, you should follow through. “Besides," she said, halfheartedly smiling, "Sha'an wouldn't want me going into danger on her account."

Blaike laughed. "But sending Aeryn in is fine?"

"Oh, of course," chimed Sip, "He always said he'd be her knight-in-shining armor."

The group burst out laughing. It was true; on multiple occasions, he had heroically announced his undying loyalty and protection, should Sha'an ever need it. Young Aeryn had been blessed with a knack for the dramatic and had made full use of it. It had likely gotten exhaustive for him, his friends, or both, because the current Aeryn was much more reserved.

Aeryn smirked, "Then I guess I don't have a choice. Let's hope you're right about your Aug room skillset. Otherwise, this is the most foolish errand that fools have ever fooled."

Sip was grinning. "Of course I'm right! And no, you don't. So, here's how I see this going..."

~ Eight ~

"Take a step. Breathe.
Take another step.
Another breath.
This is the path of Life."
Hcami Le'al, La Vida Vedic

The Ta'ak ship was scheduled to leave the following evenly, so the newly formed "crew" had to act expediently. There was no time for breakfast, in Aeryn's mind, but Sip insisted that they needed to eat.

"After all," Sip had said through a mouthful of eggs, "who knows when we might eat again?"

Aeryn struggled to finish, but eventually got through his plate. After their quick repast, the two convened one last time before parting ways until the evening.

"All you have to do is pack a light bag with a few days of clothes and hygienics," Sip reassured Aeryn. "Meet me at the alley between the landing field and the stone house."

"Where we always meet to watch ships come and go, I know," Aeryn replied. "I'll be there."

Aeryn made no detours on his return to his quarters. His small leather backpack had not seen much use since his Academy days. It showed its age in its faded appearance, but it was still strong. He picked up the luggage and beat the dust from it, opening the pockets and zippers whose insides hadn't breathed in years. Inside a zipped pocket in the main section of the pack, Aeryn found a sheaf of paper that at once lit his eyes and sunk his heart. Sha'an had been one to write notes like ancient hyumins on disposable media, even though the norm for centuries had been digital messaging. The brittle paper was filled end to end, top to bottom with thoughts and drawings. She had always been so talented with artistic implements. It is shown in the mixtures of media and style on the page, each distinct yet flowing together. The letter was from after a trip to the Riverfront they had taken during their last break before their Records Exam. It detailed, in the subtle language of inside jokes and doodles, her elation at what had happened during the outing, and the dawning realization that it may be their last one ever.

A knock brought him back to reality. It was Axly, standing in the doorframe. This was the second time in a week that she had done so, and Aeryn was overcome with a strong sense of deja vu.

"You're crying," she said.

She closed the distance and was at once wiping his tears. Aeryn handed her the note. She took it, sitting on the bed with her head down towards the note she now held in her lap. Half a smile made its way across her lips. Her eyes swelled with memories.

"Now who's crying?" Aeryn teased.

He sat next to her. She plunked her head on his shoulder.

"I don't want you to go," she said.

She wrapped her arms around one of his. They had rarely been this close before. Hugs across the years in plenty, yes, but this felt different.

"We've already lost Sha'an. If you left and didn't come back..." she trailed off, tears now springing freely from her eyes.

Aeryn leaned into her. "As long as Sip's insane plan goes at least mostly right, I should be fine. Mostly."

He looked at her, trying to convey humor and failing. She punched his arm.

"Not funny."

"You're right. I barely want to go either. I don't know what we would even be able to accomplish should we even manage to get off planet. I think Sip might be on a manic ride."

Aeryn readjusted so that both his arms were around her.

"I want to be there to make sure he doesn't go too far. And makes it home. There are myriad opportunities for failure"

He felt her head nod up and down. He lifted it so that he was looking into her eyes.

"I promise you I'll come home. Even if my body fails, my voice will find you in the whispers of the wind; my gaze will find you from the heavens; my soul will make its home in your dreams."

Their faces were close. Their lips barely touched, then fully entwined. Time ceased, there was only this.

"Aeryn! It's time to...oh," came a voice from the hall.

Aeryn and Axly separated, both their faces red having been caught so vulnerable. It was Blaike.

Blake started again to break the awkwardness. "Ax, you should go find Tymiha, she's waiting for you," then looked at Aeryn. "And Sip is probably already at the rendezvous by now. He was skiffing like his tails were on fire when we parted ways just now."

Axly got up, wiped her eyes, and nodded. She took one last look at Aeryn and mouthed two words: *come back!*

Then she left the room. A part of Aeryn left with her.

Sip was waving his hand in what could be described as a "stealthy" way, making small circles parallel to the wall in whose shadow he was crouching. Aeryn approached slowly in a normal gate, which was greeted by Sip's full eyeballs and a double-handed gesture to *get down!* Aeryn could barely contain himself as he garishly crouched down to appease his friend. Sip whipped his tongue around in an annoyed fashion, then motioned to his partner-in-crime to follow him to the far side of the ally. Once there, they sat with their hands around their bundled legs under an angled bin cover.

They sat in watchful silence until at last Sip said, "Blaike was supposed to be here by now."

As if summoned by the spoken name, a message from Blaike appeared on both their armlets:

---Running late---

Aeryn was concerned. This was a precarious enough situation as is. Sip saw this,

“Don’t worry, Anno,” he reassured Aeryn. “I have no doubt this will go swimmingly.”

"Do you ever? The ego on you, friend."

"Confidence, friend. You should get some."

"And you both need to learn to keep quiet," came Blaike's voice from outside the improvised shelter.

Three heads filled the entrance to the hovel, then they all crawled inside and sat against the wall.

"Axly almost didn’t come," said Blaike stoically. "Tymiha was going to play her part and stay behind."

Aeryn's thoughts turned to a few hours ago. He would have been relieved if she hadn’t shown up. He would have been happier that way; wouldn’t have felt the guilt he did now about making her a part of this.

All he said was "Understood," which was the opposite of true. "In which case, we need to start now. Ax, you're up."

She nodded and set off towards the ambassador's ship door. They could see her faintly in the distance as she approached.

"Okay," Sip said, "are we ready to go once they leave?"

Aeryn nodded. So did Blaike.

Any minute now.

Except the guards weren't leaving. The pair of birds just stood there, paying Axly little mind.

Axly was gesticulating wildly enough to be noticed from this far away. Just then, from another direction, the group saw an approaching Maestro hailing her. The robed figure beckoned her away from the ship. She looked at him, then the guards, then at the group, then hung her head and walked away with the Maestro.

"Now what?' asked Blaike.

Sip was thinking, eyes darting back and forth. His eyes caught something and locked on. "There," he pointed to a hatch door with a line of supplies outside.

Aeryn did not feel like saying anything about the newly ridiculous path this plan was taking, nor how Sip was endangering the plan and himself by risking getting caught, so he didn't. The worst that could happen if they were caught would be them ushered away and probably lectured on diplomacy and decorum.

Within minutes, the group was ducked among the various crates and containers outside the ship's loading bay. Aeryn was losing patience quickly.

"What now, Sip?" Aeryn whispered with annoyance.

"Now," Sip replied cooly, "we find boxes to hide in, and wait to get loaded onto the ship."

"And then how do we get out?" Blaike added.

"I've been thinking about that," said Sip, "and it would be easiest to have one of us open the boxes for the other three."

"Which one?" asked Aeryn, already knowing the answer.

"Me, of course. I'm the only one with even a chance of staying out of sight."

Blaike's face turned doubtful. "Even though you're not able to chromoflage?"

Sip bristled. "It's not that I can't, I just haven't yet!"

Blaike frowned. "That's not any better."

"Even without it, I can still remain out-of-sight in a way more rigid bodies cannot," Sip retorted.

"I'll show you rigid-"

“Alright, alright," Aeryn broke in. "Let's just find some containers."

Their search was a shorter affair than they had anticipated. Blaike found a suitable crate quickly, which almost had room for three, but they decided to not make this any more uncomfortable than it had to be. She and Tymiha took that one.

Aeryn was having much less luck, until they came to a large metal box with no writing on the outside.

Sip looked the box over. "I wonder what's inside."

There was no lock on the large clasp that held the door, and it gave easily when tugged.

Dry smoke rose from the vessel, revealing vacuum packed containers of all kinds of aquatic life.

"It must be for the kitchen," Aeryn thought out loud. "Unless they have some kind of fish-powered engine."

Sip laughed. "Let's get you inside."

Aeryn paused. "How am I supposed to breathe?"

Sip looked around. "Good question. Let's see..."

It took a few minutes, but Sip eventually found an exhaust pump with a trap to the exterior. He propped the door open with a hose.

"There we go," said Sip.

Aeryn contemplated the makeshift breathing apparatus, and the metal box that could easily become his unwitting sarcophagus. Gathering his nerve, he climbed in. The last thing he saw was the smiling face of his friend, which made him even less confident.

"See you on the other side!" said Sip, closing the lid.

Then, darkness.

~ Nine ~

"Know Thyself"

Socrates, Plato, etc
Inscription, Temple of Apollo, Greece, Old Earth

The stillness was unlike anything Aeryn had ever experienced before. Even during his meditative studies, there was always some small amount of noise. There was always the wind, if nothing else. Inside the sealed chamber, there was a silence so absolute that it felt like darkness was creating it. The silence rang in his ears until a high-pitched buzzing filled his head. His eyes squelched shut in response, but it changed nothing. The sound was mounting, echoing off his skull in a tyrannical rhythm. Pain both mental and now physical assaulted him. He wanted it to end with every ounce of his being, but it wouldn't. It was too much, and then, nothing. When Aeryn was next aware, he was sitting in a grey-green void.

Sitting wasn't the right word. Floating, maybe? That might be it. And he wasn't alone. From outside the green, as if it was a curtain, a face pushed itself into view. Was this another vision of Sha'an?

No: it looked like her, but everything was slightly off. The uncanny face of not-Sha'an donned a sickly smile, her expression too docile, her eyes reflecting nonexistent light.

Who are you?

"Everyone knows who I am, Aeryn, but who are you?"

Me? - I 'm no one special.

"And yet, you venture out, like you are one of the Seekers of knowledge. A hero of old, perhaps?"

Seeker...no. No, I'm not a hero. I'm a Reader, I keep to myself and I'm not sure what I'm doing here.

"Is that the path you chose?"

To be here?

"To be a Reader. To become a part of the Records."

I think so.

"Why do you think that?"

It made the most sense at the time. I was recommended by the Records Ambassador to the Academy.

"So you were chosen?"

Maybe? Why? Why was I chosen?

"Yes. Why you?"

I guess they thought I was a good fit.

"Do you think you're a good fit?"

I think I do my job well.

"Do you like your job?"

I like it enough. As much as someone could like a job, I supposed.

"So you haven't found joy?"

I wouldn't say that...

"Then that's why you came. You need something else."

I need to avenge my friend whose face you've stolen.

"You're the avenging type? Certainly not a trait of a Reader..."

I'm just me.

"Aeryn the Avenger."

That's not what I mean!

"Then who are you?"

I'm a guy who doesn't know what to do with the hole in his heart.

"So, this is a distraction?"

Is it?

"Is it a solution? Will doing this bring her back?"

Of course not.

"Then why?"

I'm not sure.

The twisted face of Shana morphed into a toothy, evil smile, and replied one last time:

"Let's find out together."

A sudden jolt threw Aeryn's container and a woke him from his dream. Two more followed, then a whooshing sound like air through a giant straw. The box flew across the cabin, crashing hard into the hull where oxygen was likely pouring out. There was a *SKREEEE* sound, then everything was still. Aeryn tried to move his limbs, but to no avail, his body could not shake the hold over it. Then he realized: the ship was being held in light-stasis. He and everything on board were trapped.

A slight tugging told Aeryn they were moving. Time passed without evidence. It could have been hours for all he knew. When he felt the familiar weight of gravity return, his first instinct was to get out of the container. Then, voices. He heard rhythmic scuffling as their words became clearer. They spoke the common hyumin language through thick accents. *Junons*, Aeryn thought, but it didn't make sense. How had they gotten so advanced? They barely had spacefaring technology, or at least that's what their biography said. Aeryn couldn't tell which was more unnerving, the fact that they were much more capable than previously thought, or that the Records was now twice incorrect about them.

Aeryn held his breath. There was shouting. One voice sounded like Sip, but he wasn't sure. He was sweating from his brow. It took all his willpower not to reach up and wipe it. The box holding his refrigerator was pried open. In a second, they would be on him...

"Hey tin-heads!" came a shout.

It was Sip! The commotion relocated and Aeryn was once again alone. He let out his breath cautiously, heart beating in time with the whirring alarm. After a few minutes it died down. What did that mean? Did they catch Sip? And where were Blaike and Tymiha?

He pushed at the door to his enclosure; didn't budge. His palms were sweating now. There should be an emergency open switch some in there. His hands fumbled in the pitch dark until they discovered a depression in the door. His finger probed it until he heard a *click*, then the room was alight.

Aeryn's eyes strained in the orange emergency lights. There was no sound from anywhere around. He stuck his head out just enough to see over the crate walls. Most of the other cargo had been ransacked and thrown about. He climbed out of his shelter. There was a door leading out of the cargo bay whose slider was stuck half-open. Aeryn wasted no time, spared no thought, and was out that door.

The cargo bay spilled into a vast open sphere with hallways around the circumference. The sheer size was dizzying. Aeryn clung to the railing as he felt a wave of fear wash over him. Ever so cautiously, Aeryn shuffled foot-to-foot, hand-to-hand around the gangway until he came to an alcove in the wall. Putting his back against the wall relieved the vertigo, at least somewhat, so he was able to take in his surroundings.

This could be the central chamber of a ship, or something much larger. He wasn't sure how much time had passed since they were intercepted, but they couldn't have gone that far.

I need to find Sip, he thought. As if manifesting from his words, a pained yell rang out through the hub. The sound echoed; it wasn't clear from where it had come. Aeryn's eyes darted around, his head on a swivel, then another scream identified his quarry.

Nearer the bottom of the sphere by two levels, almost directly across from him marched a stream of metal. Their forms were optimized for work as soldiers. Aeryn's heart skipped hard in his chest. He had never seen any mechanica built for taking lives. Many of the mining drones were equipped with tools that could be used as weapons, but their forms were optimized for the excavation and transportation of minerals. These were giants in comparison, and they carried weapons reminiscent of long-ago wars. In their midst were the familiar travel-robes of the Arcay being herded around the corridor towards an open hatch. What awaited inside, he couldn't imagine. That's where he had to go.

There was no obvious path to his destination, so Aeryn slunk along the railing towards the other side of the sphere. As he progressed, he noticed the intricate movements of the protocol drones occupying the vast chasm in between the ring-ways. The complex choreography followed patterns that shifted ever so in a way that it looked fluid; a graceful may-bodied beast. It was then that Aeryn had a thought only the young and the reckless would think:

Ride the wave.

The nearest-passing outbound trail of drones passed directly through the central column, which did not look like it could accommodate a biological passenger. Just before the column were access routes for what must have at one point been for manual access. Above them, another trail of drones passed through the column then dove down to the intended floor. Aeryn was not what one would call "athletic," having spent most of his life in studies, but this predicament required him to display prowess that he never had before. He took a deep breath. In the moment of its zenith, he imagined the acrobatics that Sip would perform daily back on Arc, then opened his eyes and let it out. He dashed towards the edge of the precipice as if he knew what he was doing, then flung himself over the railing.

For a moment, Aeryn's panic took hold of him. The ledge was about ten feet from the last of the drones, and he was falling fast. A wild flailing of his arms brought him in contact with the landing gear of his mark. He gripped tighter than he had ever before. Pain shot through his wrist as he struggled to maintain hold of the flying machine. The machine did not seem to notice. The additional weight was promptly accounted for, and the flight continued along its path. Aeryn managed to swing a leg up over the lander and was suspended like a sloth from it.

He adopted a more chameleon-like pose and looked for his drop point. The drones' flight pattern had altered enough that he could be closer to the column than he planned. He would have to drop a longer distance than he was confident to drop. The safest option was to see where this line took him and jump directly onto the column.

It was a column in looks only. The "structure", though non-structural, was composed of floating sheaves of what looked like metalloid ceramic surrounding a central beam of vertical light. The ceramics wound above and around each other. The movements may have had some purpose, but Aeryn couldn't add them to the pattern in any meaningful way. It was approaching fast. He had to act. He started swinging his body back and forth to gain some momentum. The column would be near enough to land on in a few seconds. He would be clear in three, two, one-

All fear left Aeryn the moment he took the plunge. The distance closed in an instant. Too quickly for a graceful landing. Aeryn hit the column like a brick. His head swam as he scraped and skidded down. His feet crashed into the platform but couldn't hold his weight, and his butt plopped hard onto the grated metal.

He shook off the shock and scrambled to his feet. There was no railing, so he gripped the edge like a gargoyle while the column rotated towards the goal.

Five more seconds, four, three...

The line of drones appeared from around the central column.

Two.

One.

Jump!

This time, he was ready, landing on two drones at once to lessen his impact. The drones continued their path, approaching the far side of the chamber. Then they stopped. Everything stopped. for a moment, you could hear the thumping of Aeryn's heart over the absolute silence.

Then they started up again, but not in the same direction as before. The drones circled the column, spiraling upward in a dizzying display. Aeryn gripped tighter. *We're going the wrong way!* He pried his face away from his metallic steed and peered downward. The distance to the bottom of the sphere was growing, and with it, Aeryn's fear of heights. He let out the tiniest of whimpers but held fast.

Approaching from the room's apex was another line of drones; only these ones were armed. He pressed himself closer to his holdfast for a moment, trying to evade detection. Then, he had a much better idea. As the drone patrol came into reach, Aeryn leapt out and kicked the lead drone. Its response was immediate; the drone and its flock all turned towards this new threat with weapons charged.

Aeryn had expected this, using the opportunity to jump to a soldier-drone in the middle of the flight pattern. It crashed into a neighbor, discharging a weapon in the process. The ensuing chaos was enough to set off another blaring alarm, this time coming from the drones themselves. Their green lights turned to whirring yellow ones as they reformed from individual lines to a complex grid-like pattern that moved in circles around the central column. Aeryn had not expected that.

This new pattern presented new problems, but also much better opportunities for mobility. The soldier-drones would be the biggest issue, but they were still in calamity after seemingly being assaulted by one of their own. He hoped that would be enough to buy him the time he needed to descend the throngs of moving mechanica. The spacing between each was at least two meters, and getting enough momentum to jump horizontally from one to the next would be difficult on the easily swayed hovering machines. He would have to jump down and out. It looked like that would give him enough outward distance to reach the closer, lower decks of the sphere where he wanted to be. If there was a faster way, he didn't see it.

Aeryn shifted his grip so that he was holding the landing gear and facing away from the column. With a few swings for confidence, he flung himself forward, doing something of a flip in the hangtime. His ungraceful first attempt got him to his destination, but almost found him slipping off into the abyss below. The next was a little better, and the third nearly picturesque. The fourth presented a challenge. There was no "next" drone for at least twenty meters downwards. Around him, drones were returning to their previous patterns, and the soldier drones were descending again. He had no choice. Situating himself on top of his current vessel, Aeryn took a deep breath, then stepped forward...

...onto nothing. The drone had shifted under him and he was now tumbling through the air. He couldn't right himself. He had nothing to grab onto. There was only the inevitable down.

CRACK

Aeryn lost his breath as he collided with an outbound drone, alone in its travels, unlike the others. It was as if this drone had been set along this path with him in mind, as it was heading directly towards the door Aeryn needed. Within the space of a minute, Aeryn was to the side of the sphere again, feeling safer now with the floor underneath him. Behind him, the vast space felt like a barrier between lifetimes. His purpose was renewed. He ran through the door with the confidence of someone who knew what he was doing, even though he lacked the knowledge. He was rounding a corner corridor when a strange light caught his attention.

The source room was an unguarded one, empty besides a few terminals attached to a plinth in their center. There was something on the plinth that looked strangely familiar. It was a feeling like seeing a bird inside a building: you know what it is, but you don't know why it's here. He felt himself drawn to it, his curiosity getting the better of him. A faint light pulsed inside the object as he approached. *That's it!* He couldn't contain his surprise as the realization dawned on him:

A knowledge crystal!

~ Ten ~

"Careless hearts in unknown lands find graves under their shifting sands"

Naheki Hunting Rhyme

Aeryn couldn't believe his eyes. Of all the places to come across the most sought-after substance in the universe, his captors' ship was the last place he would have thought this could happen.

No, that makes sense. Why target Arcays unless for our most precious resource?

He would have to finish that thought later. The rock beckoned him closer, and he had no mind to resist. As he drew closer, the room seemed to darken, until there was only he and the glowing treasure.

"You came."

Aeryn nearly tripped over himself in surprise. He looked around. Nothing. Just darkness. Not even the rest of the ship was visible, let alone this shrouded speaker.

"Who's there?"

The crystal flashed before him. Aeryn gazed into it. The light was almost blinding, but deep inside it...a shadow.

Aeryn's hand was reaching out towards the warm, inviting glow. He laid it upon the crystal. Everything went white.

Aeryn looked around. He was in a white room, well-appointed with furniture of leather and marble of the snowiest whites, draped with furs and smatterings of pillows.

"Most Welcome, Aeryn Anno. Most Welcome."

On the far side of the room, beside a particularly large chair, stood a figure unlike any Aeryn had seen before. What he could see of it, that is: it had large antlers like those of an Old Earth deer, and two arms and two legs that fit into a suit like a regular human would. Its face was Annother mystery altogether. It shifted.

Not between different human faces, but between everything. Animals, humans, paintings, concepts, feelings; it was the face of something not wholly itself, nor quite anything else.

"Come. Sit."

The being gestured towards a couch nearest the large chair, into which it settled down. Aeryn regarded the offer with suspicion, then realized he had no other option. With a great deal of reluctance, he approached and sat. He was within arms reach of the entity now. It was much larger up close and had a quality to it like an aura of sound. Indistinguishable noises seem to emanate from it. Aeryn began.

"Who are you?" Then, after a moment, "We've spoken before."

"We have, child, yes. We met first when your mind slipped into the Void, and we spoke again very recently. As to who I am, that is not for now. You don't know enough yet. It would mean nothing to you."

"But you brought me here for a reason?"

"Quite the opposite. I invited you hoping to find the reason."

"That makes no sense."

"Sense isn't something that's made, it's found. And you would do well to find some of yours, young Anno. You've become brash. Does this have to do with...her?"

Aeryn bristled. "Don't talk about her."

"So it is. And likely always will be, no matter how far from it you stray. Old wounds stay with us. Old scars never disappear."

It paused.

"Do you know much about the Records?"

Aeryn thought for a second, then responded "I do. We cover their history in our studies, so it's common knowledge."

"Enlighten me."

"Millenia ago, Hyumins, then called 'humans" discovered a crystalline substance out in the far reaches of our home galaxy, which they called The Milky Way." He laughed. "Funny name; anyway, after finding the first of the crystals, hyumins found that other species from different planets also had discovered shards of these same crystals in their systems.

This lead to the Cooperative of Sentience, wherein three planets allied themselves in search of these crystals. From the knowledge within, we have learned much about the nature of the universe, and so we study and collect them. We've been collecting and sharing knowledge since then."

"Bravo, Aeryn," the entity responded. **"You certainly have an aptitude for memorization. The Reader mantle suits you well. Almost as well as...never mind. And do you believe this story?"**

This was what Aeryn expected to be asked of him, and he was ready. "Yes. I have no doubt, nor reason to doubt."

"No reason? What about your recent discovery? The...discrepancy?"

He had almost forgotten. But it was at the forefront of his mind now, and he couldn't just let it go again.

"I see. So there is a reason. Let me cast you some light; The story is mostly true. It seems you know the beginning of when your kind became part of the story of the crys-

tals, but not of anything beforehand, nor after their fall from relevance."

"And are you going to tell me?"

"Again, no, and for the same reason. But I will tell you this: there are still those alive who know the answer. One may be a Maestro, or even a Promnus, in your order."

Aeryn blinked. "...a Maestro?"

The being smiled, or at least what could be called a smile on his face-of-many-things. Then he was gone. The room was gone. Everything was gone.

Aeryn was back in the crystal chamber. His hand was still grasping the stone. He seized it back, turned, and ran from the chamber. He stopped outside, looking from left to right, having no idea where to go.

[Left]

Not stopping to think about the ramifications of the voice in his head, Aeryn took off leftwards. He was heading towards a gear-shaped door that was locked in place by a series of bolts. He would have to guess at how to-

It opened. The security light turned a vibrant blue as lengths of energy undid the bolts, after which the door turned into place, receded into the wall, then split down the center. Whatever was on the other side must be important.

The shadows parted to reveal a long corridor, illuminated by nothing more than three strips of pale orange light. His eyes adjusted as he entered, allowing him to see that the hall was lined with smaller chambers. Some were larger than others, but none more than six arms across, all enclosed by seamless, transparent panes. Compared to the other chambers, this one felt almost hyumin in design. Or at least with hyumins in mind.

He found out why.

There were only a few occupied compartments, and at least two were filled with sentient beings, about ten to a cell. Aeryn saw hyumins and Ta'ak among them, and members of planets he'd only heard of: two Rhotohedrons, a trio of Untritia (as their kind are three-bodied, this was probably one person to them), and one last soul that made Aeryn's heart leap.

A Rrelt!

Aeryn had seen a few Rrelt, and of course he knew of Thrum, but only from a distance, and in their formal suits. Without the armor, their diminutive form was a whole different experience. Their large heads and arms connected to a comparatively smaller torso, ending in thick stubs of feet, and not much in terms of legs in between.

"Aeryn!" came a call from the next cell over. He turned to see Blaike waving frantically, surrounded by other faces both familiar and new. Tymiha and Luc were there too, but Sip was still nowhere to be found. Hopefully that meant he was still undetected. The Ta'ak delegation had been separated from their leader, who was also missing, leaving the young guards anxiously picking at their feathered claws.

"Blehey!" Aeryn shouted unintelligibly. He was too excited to form real words, but the sentiment was enough. He ran to the control panel just inside the hallway and tried to make sense of the panel. It wasn't like anything they had back on Arc, nor like anything he'd seen come through Physical Archive.

"It's a bioreactive neuropad!" yelled Tymiha, seeing Aeryn's confusion. "Put your hand on it and think about what you want to do!"

How convenient, thought Aeryn. A second thought opened the doors to his friends, then a third opened the door to the other sentients.

The other two occupied cells contained each a single inhabitant. A lithe, muscular animal lay quiet in one. It regarded Aeryn momentarily, then returned to its resigned position. The second might have seemed empty except for a wooden barrel to the untrained eye, but Aeryn recognized the container. The marks were in a language he didn't know, but the warning was clear, this was a dangerous botanical specimen. Most likely it was a giant Garish Bloom. The barrel was probably to inhibit light from reaching it, else it might grow unfathomably. How- or why it was here on this ship was a mystery that Aeryn didn't have time to decipher.

In the three seconds it took to notice all that, Aeryn's friends were upon him in a clumsy group embrace. He genuinely loved them, as they did him. He hadn't appreciated them like this since before Sha'an died.

They broke apart and formed a huddle, flanked by the other captives.

"First, has anyone seen Sip, and second, what's the plan?" asked Aeryn.

Tymiha shrugged, "Not since he packed us up in the cargo bay." Blaike shook their head. Luc said nothing.

"Luc, how did you get here?" Aeryn asked. "Did you get Axly's message?"

"I did," he replied, "then I passed it on to Thrum and grabbed the first shuttle out that I could. I got intercepted and wound up here."

"At least we're all here together. Finding Sip is our first priority," Aeryn declared. "But we also need to figure out how to get out of here. Where even are we?"

"The ship that dragged us in was pretty big, so this must be some kind of hub," offered Luc.

"The gravity is only artificial inside the halls, maybe it's a moon base?" said Tymiha.

"Probably not a moon," chimed Blaike. "we're not near any planets, it could be an aster."

The group nodded in agreement.

"Right," said Aeryn, "then there could be other ports besides the one we came in." Then he had an idea. "Escape pods. Assuming there are living beings stationed here, there must be some. Or there were some at some point. The only staffing I've seen has been robotic."

"Great, but what do we do about Sip?" asked Tymiha. "Should we split up an look for him?"

It was then that the Rrelt spoke up.

"We should stay together. There are already too few of us to hold against the full might of this enclave, and splitting our number won't do anything to improve that."

Aeryn was not sure how to tell Rrelt genders, but this one might be the less masculine one. Rrelt biology is known to doctor-surgeons and few others but was a matter of great secrecy even within the Halls of Arc. Aeryn wouldn't have known how to address them even with that knowledge, so he chose to use their formal title when one meets a new person.

"Yes, sera. My name is Aeryn, and these are Blaike, Tymiha, and Luc. We're from Arc. What can we call you?"

"You got 'sera' right, I'll commend you for that. My identisound is *Nnvnva*, though Niva would be fine for Irrelti."

The group looked at Niva blankly.

Niva laughed. "Non-Rrelt. Those who don't primarily use their vibrating jawbone to speak. I can speak UniCom, but as I get older, I may require the translation devices that some of our more lockjawed citizens communicate with."

She turned to Aeryn. "I'm not surprised even a Reader like yourself didn't know. We keep weaknesses to ourselves, no matter how slight."

Aeryn smiled. "Then I am sure happy to have met you. Do you have any idea where we might start?"

Niv shook her head, which in her case was more like a full- body wag.

"I was brought in through the same port everybody else was. I hate to say, but that might also be the best way out."

"It doesn't make sense to backtrack all that way when that's exactly where they expect us to go," said Luc. "And we should do some investigating while we're here. We -are- Record Keepers, after all."

Aeryn was mildly annoyed that Luc's suggestion made sense and kept with their creed, but not everyone was a Record Keeper. Before he could think to respond, Tymiha was at the neuropad. After a few seconds, she looked up.

"There are escape pods, down near the base of the sphere. We should be able to get to them from the elevators at the next hallway over. They don't seem to be in use."

Behind her, the door slid open, revealing two guards. Their mostly robotic faces still showed signs of humanity.

"You are out of compliance. Return to your cells," said the one nearest Tymiha, raising his weapon arm at her. The look of terror on her face spread around the room as the weapon charge filled...

TSEWW!

The robot's weapon had not discharged. It looked down at its weapon arm to find it missing; strewn upon the ground, with a gaping hole where it had been attached. It tried to respond and fell over. Someone was behind it, sending chills across Aeryn's skin.

"Sip!" he yelled. The remaining guard turned to face the new threat; weapon charged.

That was all the opening Niva needed. She vaulted toward the remaining guard, two arms latching to its torso, the other two to its weapon arm. With a sound like a revving engine and the shredding of gears, Niv ripped the arm out of its socket. She tossed it aside, gripped the cyborg's robotic skull cover, and slammed her fourth hand into its bionic face until it fell underneath her assault.

This spectacular show of violence was undercut by Sip's appearance. He had shed his robes to the waist, tying the arms around them, and, most surprisingly, wielding a military-class blaster. Aeryn raced forward to embrace his friend.

"Sip, my dearest friend," Aeryn was practically weeping, "You are the cleverest of all of us, aren't you?" Tears swelled at the edges of his eyes.

Sip just flashed his trademark half-smile. "I keep trying to tell you all."

"Where'd you get the blaster?" asked Luc, suddenly right next to them.

"Picked it up off a guard. Well, almost picked. It caught me halfway through and I had to rough it up a little bit." He paused. "I mean it was a robot, so it had to crush it until it stopped beeping."

Aeryn burst out laughing. It was the best he'd felt in ages. He felt like he could take the whole station by himself.

"We've got to get to the escape pods now," he said, then looked at the Ta'ak guards. "Do you know where your leader was taken?"

One with a red plume between his eyes stepped forward. "We don't, but it was nearer the top of the sphere."

The other, a fully grey specimen, clearly of seniority, added, "Do not concern yourself with Ta'ak business, you have done us service enough, young stowaways." It bowed low, as did the first.

Aeryn and Sip returned their bows, and the Ta'ak departed, stopping first at the neuropad, then exiting through the door to the sphere. Niv collected the weapons from the downed guards and handed them to Aeryn and Luc.

"One day maybe I'll teach the two of you to fight properly. Until then, you'll probably need these," she said with a smirk.

Luc accepted eagerly. He looked down the sight and feigned blasting sounds, then held it like a soldier at ease would. Aeryn looked at the rifle and then at Sip.

"Trade me?" he asked.

"Pleassse," replied Sip. "This thing is a little touchy, so keep off the trigger unless you're using it."

"Thanks, will do," said Aeryn, then addressed the group. "Let's move."

They moved to the anterior door, where Annother neuropad was set into the wall. It opened with a thought, and the two disappeared. Aeryn felt concern for them, then let it go.

Sip led the group towards the door, brandishing his new armament, followed by Luc, then Tymiha and Blaike, with Aeryn and Niva bringing up the rear.

~ Eleven ~

"We don't have much here, but we do have each other, and that keeps us happy."

Recordant Unknown
Recording 10830.877.009, Gronwei Personal Archives

The hallway was alive with activity. Buzzing from the drones above almost masked the blaring alarm, and there was another tone. Lower, rhythmic, thudding. The band found themselves in the path of two columns of armed guards, now readying their weapons at the sight of the escapees.

Sip reacted like a veteran soldier, loosing a blast from his rifle into the closest, then another into the one behind it. Luc fumbled for a second, but then was able to crack off a blast that downed the next closest borg. Aeryn hadn't raised his handblaster at all, still not sure about using it. He knew these robotic creatures were not biological, but it didn't mean that they deserved lethal judgment. Whatever was controlling them was causing their deaths, not Aeryn. The beings they were had already died when they were assimilated.

He knew Blaike noticed this, by the way she put her hand on his shoulder and took the blaster.

"It's okay. I'll handle this," she said in a warm, reassuring tone. Compared to the cacophony around them, it was a silken song on a breeze.

Aeryn and Tymiha stayed tight behind their armed allies. Niva had already joined in the rabble, punching and crushing the mechanical ops in front of her. She had gathered up rifles from fallen guards and was now tetra-wielding blasters at the enemies around her.

"Tymiha!" she called, "I need some height!"

Reading the intention exactly, Tymiha burst from behind Aeryn and crouched down. Niva vaulted herself onto Tymi's back and plopped her little legs over Tymi's shoulders. Raised up, they were a formidable sight.

Aeryn was now the only one not actively participating in the battle and felt like he needed to do something, though there wasn't much to do.

"Aeryn!" It was Sip. "There's more coming around, we can't do this forever!"

"Run to the elevators! I'll distract them!" he shouted back.

"But..." Sip stopped, then nodded, smiling. "Go be the hero, you animal."

Animal. He had an idea. "New plan! I'll be right back!"

Aeryn shot him back a look of false bravado, then took off towards the cell hallway they had just exited. A blast hit the adjacent wall and his ears rang like church-bells. The next few steps were agonizing.

Once inside, Aeryn stumbled down until he was in front of the cell holding the creature.

It perked up its head, now seeing Aeryn for the second time. It eyed him warily, then, with some effort, rose itself off the floor. Its features were like those of an Old Earth panther but exaggerated in size and musculature. There were also the additional front appendages and long chest, lending the beast an almost centaur-like quality. It approached on all six, then sat on its haunches and heightened its chest. Then it raised a hand.

Greeting

It could talk! Moreso, it could talk telepathically, which would have surprised Aeryn if he hadn't had so many other voices in his head recently.

"I'm going to open the door," he said, with no regard to whether he could trust this being.

Please yes

"And you won't hurt me?"

No hurt. Friend now. Mrow.

Mrow? Was that a noise or its name?

It is name. And noise. Then audibly, **"Mrowww."**

"I'm Aeryn Anno, from the Opal Moon Arc," he said, touching the neuropad and unlocking the cell. Mrow trod gracefully out of his enclosure and up to Aeryn. It was quite a sight to behold up close like this.

Climb on and we move faster.

Aeryn couldn't contain his happiness, a broad grin spreading on his face.

AAAAAAAAAAAAAAAAAAAAA!!!!!

Mrow's limbs beat out a rhythm like thunder echoing off the metal corridors. Aeryn had never moved this fast before. Ground transport on Arc was deliberate and timely, but never speedy. This was like an open-air speeder, and it was exhilarating! Mrow moved like lighting from one guard to the next, claws flashing through the air, rending metal like paper.

How did they even trap it in the first place?

Aeryn heard a response in his head: ***Big trap, made for heliphants.***

Aeryn had never seen a heliphant before, but he could fathom their comparative size, and it made sense.

In a matter of seconds, they were barreling down the corridor to the elevators. His friends were cornered but holding, pinned against the elevators by a swarm of drones and guards. But not for long.

Aeryn dismounted and fired into the metallic masses. Two guards went down, catching the attention of the drones, which redirected their efforts in his direction. They were quickly brought down by Mrow's overwhelming assault, until none remained. It was only then that Aeryn realized that the halls had emptied, and the alarm had ceased.

"This was by far your best plan yet, hero," said Sip, looking around, "but this sudden calm is enervating."

Aeryn nodded. "Then it's time to – AHk!" Aeryn grabbed his head, trying to contain the pressure that had overtaken it.

Aeryn

Again with this. We *just* talked.

Aren't you forgetting something?

No?

You're just going to leave the crystal?

Oh. No! Wait. Yes? Why does it matter to you?

You're a Record Keeper, it's your charge

This was a good point, but Aeryn kept that out of his mind's dialogue.

That's not what I asked.

He felt a rumbling in his skull like boiling laughter.

And I'm not answering that. Retrieve the crystal, and your friends will have a clear escape path. And before you try to barter for the Ta'ak, they've already escaped

Something was not right, but the deal was to their immediate benefit. Aeryn opened his eyes to find he was on the floor, the others surrounding him in a huddle. He sat up, still dizzy.

"Are you okay?" It was Tymiha, pulling a tincture out of her bag. "Come here, smell this."

Aeryn took a whiff that sent him rushing back to his senses.

"Wow, thanks. I'm fine, but I must do something." Aeryn said, getting to his feet.

Sip made a hissy sound. "It's always something with you."

"I swear it'll only take a few minutes, but it's important. You can get everybody to the escape pods without me, right?"

Blaike interjected. "And how exactly are you going to get out?"

Aeryn tried to say something, then the words got caught in his throat. He hadn't planned that far ahead. Niva spoke up.

"I think I can get us out. There's a Rrelt miner in the hangar. Assuming we can get to it, I can pilot us out," she said.

"What about the hoards of mechanica? We barely made it past the few we ran into," argued Luc.

"I don't think they're going to be much more of a problem," replied Aeryn. When everybody kept silent, he continued, "I think their attention is elsewhere."

"Even if that was the case, we can't just leave you!" cried Tymiha. Her concerns were genuine, as were those of the others. Aeryn was lucky to have them. It was only at this moment that he thought that he could possibly lose them. Moisture welled up in the corners of his eyes.

“You guys are the best, but we need to start making decisions,” he said. "Mrow and Niva will come with me, the rest of you, get out safely. We’ll see each other again soon.”

With palpable reluctance, the others boarded the elevators. Aeryn turned around before they could see the tears start to fall.

Niva and Aeryn mounted the majestic Mrow and set off back towards the main expanse. They had just reached the sphere’s edge when Niva made a request.

“I think we should stop back at the cells one more time,” she said. “That plant-in-a-barrel gave me an idea.”

Aeryn looked at her, puzzled, then enlightenment came, and a grin spread across his face.

“If you’re thinking what I’m thinking, then I’m in,” he replied.

The doors had all been opened, and the drones returned to their patterns. It was like the Voice said, the path was clear. He could only hope his friends were having this easy a time.

Niva dismounted, then retrieved the container from its now-ajar compartment, her two "front" arms free while the much more muscular back arms clamped the barrel.

"Are you going to be able to carry all this, Mrow?" she asked before mounting again.

Yes, yes. Not too much for Mrow.

They were on their way out again, now encircling the main sphere, looking for a path. The safe choice was to encircle the column via the outer walkways, then find an elevator to get them upwards. The problem was, this was a sphere room, which meant the only point where the bottom met the top was the central column.

"I got down here by riding the drones, maybe we can get back up that way?" Aeryn suggested.

Niva scanned the space above them. "If we can make it to the central column, we can shed some of the weight," she said, tapping the barrel. "That's as far as this lil guy needs to go."

We go now. Up up. Mrow lowered his backmost haunches and Niva hopped up.

The world became a blur. Mrow charged towards the edge with astounding speed. Aeryn was clinging so tightly that he couldn't see where Mrow was bolting towards. Anxiety and stomach acid rose in him. In an instant, Mrow had leapt off the walkway, now gliding through the air like it belonged there. The gravity well in the ship was at its densest here, but Mrow treated it like a suggestion rather than a law of physics.

The great beast barely touched each drone, bounding from one to another in a glorious display of athleticism and logistics. In a few moments, they were at the central column, a few floors down from where they needed to be. Niva dismounted again, setting down the barrel.

She got to work unstrapping each of the pressure locks. The transporters had taken extra care not to leave anything to chance, so it took Niva a few m to undo all of them. Aeryn had also gotten off Mrow but was still holding on to it. The thought struck Aeryn that he had been referring to Mrow as “it” this whole time, an was not sure that was sufficient anymore. He turned to Mrow, who was already looking at him.

Mrow is the birth-giver. Mrow has given many births before they caught Mrow. “It” is fine. We do not use little names like “it,” just our calling names. I know "she" as well.

This made Aeryn a little less anxious. *Thank you,* he thought. Mrow nodded and tapped her chest with two digits. He did the same, which made Mrow’s long, tapered ears pop up in delight.

“All finished,” called Niva. “As soon as I dump this into the column, we need to go. Are we ready?”

Aeryn and Mrow both nodded.

“Good, let’s get this pony to the show.” She tossed the large metal barrel like it was a child’s playball, then launched herself onto Mrow. “NOW! MOVE!”

Mrow was off again, and the world became a slow-motion blur around them. They were about halfway up when the sound of wrenching metal echoed through the chamber. Then there was a pop, and a ripping sound like a robotic shriek, then nothing. Mrow launched upwards one final time and they were on the platform. Aeryn looked back over the edge to see if anything had happened. Then came a rumbling sound like a stampede in the distance. Aeryn could see something blocking out the light from the column but couldn't' make out what it was. Suddenly, it was all too clear.

The Garrish Bloom lived up to its name in many ways. The foremost was becoming the largest organism in its intended environment, which was about to be on full display. Thc column of light was more than enough energy to set off the reaction. Stalks and vines broke through the massive blocks, attaching themselves to the walkways as the stem grew higher and higher. Aeryn jumped back just as a tendril latched onto the wall he clung. The stem began to bulge, then erupted into a yellow-spotted, magenta bulb, which spread as wide as the space would allow.

A tug from Mrow brought him back to reality. He tore his gaze away while the Garrish Bloom continued to wreak havoc. Any attention that they had previously garnered from the swarms of droids was now diverted to the expanding mass now taking up most of the sphere. The three had to pick up the pace as the walkway started to give under the weight of vines, which then covered the entirety of the outer walls.

They had just gotten to the bay when Aeryn remembered why he came back this way. He tapped Mrow to get her attention."Hold up for a second, I just have to duck in here," he announced.

Niva and Mrow looked at him like he had ten heads. "

We have to go NOW," answered Niva. "This thing is going to rip apart the whole place!"

This is important, yes, but Aeryn, be quick. It is more important to live than to achieve.

Mrow's thought-voice weighed heavily with concern. Aeryn just smiled. This being he met less than an hour ago cares for him already.

"I'll just be a moment," he said, dismounting and bounding towards the door. "Get to the bay and start up a ship, I'll be right behind you!"

Aeryn turned away and saw the door ajar, as if expecting him. *Of course it's expecting me. We wouldn't have made it back if it wasn't.* He half-expected to be greeted by the nightmare creature he spoke with earlier. It wasn't there; no assault of voices, no guards, nothing.

The crystal floated in front of him. This whole room hadn't seemed affected by the botanical onslaught happening outside. *Maybe it's powered by the crystal,* he thought. Aeryn reached out to take the suspended stone. He winced as his hand crossed the barrier of light that surrounded it but was surprised to find it was warm and welcoming. His hand felt lighter in the glow, then he closed his hand around the stone.

His body froze. Unable to move, he saw the world around him fade and become something completely different.

Around him was a planet untouched, serene and peaceful. There was no technology to be seen, but the trees grew as if shepherded into place. The blue-green waves of grass that swathed the fields between gave off a soft whistling sound like a flock of faraway birds. Jutting up from between the grass were familiar stones.

Opals! The plains were dotted with them; some towering structures while others were diminutive speckles. For a moment, he felt at home.

The scene changed: there were now small beings, only very early in their lives, each touching a crystal and then laughing. The opals glowed when touched, something Aeryn had not seen on Arc. He wondered what they were being shown. The scene faded to black.

A new vision appeared, this one in the darkness of space, lit by the stars. Suddenly, a streak of light passed before Aeryn, gargantuan in size but sleek in form. It barreled past him, turning him around to behold a giant planet. A sense of familiarity washed over him as he took in the immensity of the subject. It was solidified when the roving object collided with the planet. It hit with such speed that it lanced through the surface like a knife through cheese, splitting it perfectly at the seams. Enlightenment struck Aeryn. *This is the Twin Planet. I've stared up at this my entire life.* The two sides split, allowing the molten core to escape into the cold of space, winding around the waning gravity well of the ruptured supergiant, creating the great chain that bound them together. It was a sight that brought Aeryn to tears. The celestials seem so timeless, and yet here he witnessed their creation.

Again, the world dissolved, then resolved into a new landscape. This one was much more recent. It showed hyumin explorers, far from their home world, but close enough that you could see it. Their ships were primitive, mostly made up of modular compartments in series, and one large shuttle that Aeryn had only seen in the Records. The hyumins in bulky atmosphere suits were gathered around something. It was another opal shard, lodged in the crust of this otherwise barren red desert. They looked at it in awe, each probing it with tools and touching it in turn. It also glowed, but not as prominently.

The vision dimmed to darkness, then he was back in the bay, holding the crystal in one hand.

"AERYN, NOW!" yelled Niva from behind him. He bolted upright and sprinted to the door.

"I thought you had gone," he said.

"I couldn't leave you behind, you were taking too long, and I thought something had happened," she explained. "Mrow is already in the ship."

The hallways outside were nearly destroyed. Niva and Aeryn jumped from beam to beam navigating the detritus and growth. They climbed through a hole created by the vines wedging their way through every nook and cranny of the structure.

Ahead of them, the ramp to a small mining ship was down and waiting for them. Aeryn could see Mrow through the glass enclosure to the pilot's seat, making frantic gestures at them. A metallic wrenching sound grew louder behind them, then -

BOOM

The doors to the bay burst open, no longer able to withstand the pressure of the Garrish vines. The wall separating the sphere from the bay followed, crumpling like paper. Aeryn could see that the Bloom had taken up all the whole sphere and was about to rip the roof off it. In hindsight, the Bloom might have created a larger problem than it solved, but Aeryn wasn't concerned about that. His friends must have gotten off by now, and hopefully so had the Ta'ak delegation.

HURRY HURRY HURRY

They were close enough that Mrow's thought-voice was coming through clearly. They hit the ramp, which started to retract just as their feet landed on it. The path closed behind them, now cramped into the tiny compartment, probably only meant for a single pilot and their belongings. Niva climbed over Mrow and into the pilot seat. She tapped buttons and eased a lever into place. The engines fired up and they began skidding across the bay floor.

"Not quite...just a few adjustments...AHA!"

Niva found the button she was seeking and hammered it with her fist. It crackled and buzzed, but must have done something, because the ship was now flying towards the external bay door.

"The shield is still up!" Aeryn bellowed, pointing to the reflective sheen across the exit.

"Then we're just going to have to break through!" Niva said, tapping a screen. The mining ship's drill burst screaming to life, sparks flying as it collided with airborne debris. Another tap and the drill brightened, giving off some kind of energy.

"This should get us through the field, but it's not going to be the most pleasant experience," warned Niva. Aeryn threw his arms around Mrow, who wrapped two or hers around him. They braced for impact-

-and it never came. Aeryn peeked his head up to look. They were skimming through open space, clear of the doors by a great distance.

"What happened?" Aeryn asked Niva.

"I'm not sure," she replied. "The shield shut off right as we were about to pass through it." She powered off the drill. "We've got some kind of luck behind us."

Luck, Aeryn thought. *Or something much worse.*

~ Twelve ~

"What happens next is up to us. Be it the beginning or the end of our civilization, the burden of responsibility is ours."

Ta'ak General Klepp ak-Marikas,
Recount of The Battle of Seven Kings

Aeryn looked behind them to catch a glimpse of pursuit and found nothing. Instead, he saw the Garrish Bloom, now fully matured, in place of the aster base that one stood. Its enormity could not be conceived of by one comparatively so small. The petals had grown to ten times the width of the initial bulb, unfurling into the darkness like a pastel sailcloth.

It was only then that the ship's scanner started to beep.

"Something is coming from below," said Niva. "Hang on."

Her hand swiped the screen and the ship veered sideways, narrowly dodging a jet-black object.

"What was that?" cried Aeryn.

"THAT, I do not know, but we need to get away from it." Niva took the controls in her two front arms and fastened operated the screens with her two back arms. It hurt Aeryn's head to think about using that many arms at the same time. She was very impressive.

The object turned around on its axis as if Physics had no burden on it. It was able to keep up with them even with Niva's acrobatic maneuvering. A familiar pressure crept into Aeryn's head.

Aeryn

Oh no

Oh yes, Aeryn. Come with me. I can answer every question you have about your souvenir. You want to know, don't you?

This is why you let us live!

Correct. I still have need of you. And you want to know. You want to know about the Crystals. And you want to know about YOURSELF.

...

Aeryn

No

AERYN

NO!

Aeryn shook off the Voice. He was still being held by Mrow, who was staring at him. She must have understood what had happened.

A blast rocked the ship, throwing the catlike Mrow across the interior. Luckily for Aeryn, the graceful Mrow was quick to adjust to the throw, landing softly on the wall, like it was her choice to do so in the first place.

Then you and your friends will die.

I thought you "still had need of" me.

My plans will be delayed, but I will find another.

Another blast shook the vessel. Sparks flew from the instrument panel. Niva banged on a malfunctioning screen.

"This thing is going to fall apart if that thing keeps shooting at us," she said, exasperated. This was the closest thing Aeryn had seen to hopelessness from her.

Aeryn looked at Mrow and thought very deliberately.

Mrow nodded back. She uncurled her arms and set him down, then took a step backwards.

Niva turned around. "What are you two doing?" she asked, just as Aeryn took a step backwards and hit the cargo door button.

"Wait, Aeryn!" Niva called through the heavy carbon steel doors. That was the last thing he heard; her words blocked by the barrier between them.

He looked through the glass portcullis and said, "I'll be fine," knowing full well they couldn't hear him, nor would he likely be fine. With that, he punched the cargo release button and jettisoned into space.

I knew you would make the correct choice.

Aeryn stood silently in the small compartment. He had no idea what would happen to him, floating helplessly in space. By his shallow breaths, he realized he would probably run out of oxygen soon. In the corner there was a single space suit that looked like it was for a Rrelt. Not being of Rrelt morphology himself, Aeryn disconnected the air tank and set it slightly open. At least that way there would be some fresh air for a while, if only enough to carry his sleeping body somewhere.

His thoughts turned back to the present as he was basked in the red-orange glow of light suspension. He tried to remain calm, to be strong, but his heart was beating too fast, his mind racing with possibilities. What would happen to him? Would he ever see home again? Were his friends safe? The answers wouldn't come, though he feared they might be made real all too soon.

POP

Aeryn heard the noise like a bubble popping from inside his container. He pressed against the lone portcullis to try to see what had made it.

POP...POPOP...POPOPOPOP

Chills flew through Aeryn's body.

The Ta'ak had arrived.

A dozen Ta'ak scout fighters had dropped out of subspace, flying in determined formation like cavalry cresting a hill. *These are short-range fighters...which must mean...*

POP

The heavens disappeared behind a mountain of machinery. Articulating rows of connected chambers surrounded a hivelike mass of wound titanium, gleaming radiant courage. The Ta'ak Battle-Nest was a humbling sight.

The nearest of the scouts screamed past Aeryn's view, volleying blasts at the dark ship from repeating beam turrets. Aeryn's container rocked from the impact, but he was still caught in the light's hold. He felt a tug on his container as his captor moved to evade the next assault. From what little he could see, Aeryn knew that his escort was shielded by a dense energy web. The Ta'ak ships continued to attack, but they couldn't penetrate the shield. The dark envoy was gaining momentum. It might not be able to outrun the Ta'ak's agile mechanisms, but that shield wasn't going anywhere.

A beam shot forth from the ebon cruiser. Its path warped the space around it. *Is that some kind of gravity beam?* The confirmation came abruptly: the beam created a lightless sphere some distance ahead of them, which could only be its escape route. *If that shield can withstand wormhole travel, there was no way those beams are getting through.*

They would be at the portal in moments. Aeryn sat down. He took the crystal out of his satchel and turned it over in his hands. *All this for a chunk of rock.* He looked up towards the window, trying to take in the stars, just in case this was the last time he'd see them. He put the crystal away and focused his thoughts inward. Visions of his friends crossed his mind. *They're probably fine.* The escape pods must have been seen, and Niva and Mrow were more than capable of handling themselves. This calmed Aeryn's mind to the point where he could momentarily relax. Acceptance is bliss.

BOOM

The impact sent Aeryn into the far wall. His head collided with metal, vision swimming from the concussive force. He stumbled to the window. Outside, he saw the other half of his vessel clinging to his captor's ship, drilling into the spot where the light-hold emerged. *NIVA!* It flickered and dimmed. Aeryn felt its hold release. He was still hurtling towards the black hole, but at least he was free of his bonds.

A shadow passed in front of his viewport, for just long enough that he noticed. Aeryn looked around for what had made it, then it passed by again. He squinted through the pain and saw it was heading right for him. A magnificent metal eagle, wings spread out across the skies, reaching forth with talons towards him. Aeryn smiled. He was saved.

His mind withdrew, and Aeryn slunk into a rest unlike any he'd had before.

~ Thirteen ~

"There can be no greater pride nor pleasure than to see the efforts of your teaching find its place in the next generation."

Seyj Iyden
Canticles of Iyden

There was a buzzing sound, and bright lights. A beeping sound. Rhythmic, slow. There was another person there. Maybe more?

Aeryn brought his hands to his face and squeezed. He felt bandages; his head was still sore. There was another person in the room. Maybe two? He wiped his eyes and attempted to open them. Too much light, too much headache.

"He's up!"

He knew that voice. It was one of his friends. Sip! Forgetting the pain, he sat upright too quickly, falling back onto the pillow immediately.

"Stay down, soldier," said Sip. "You've been through enough."

Aeryn adjusted so that he could make some eye contact.

"Did we get everyone out?" he asked, voice cracking through parched lips.

The answer came in a circle of heads appearing in his view. He smiled.

"Not too bad for your first rescue, hero." Sip said, grinning as well.

"There are still more Arcay to be brought home, but now that the Ta'ak fleet is in control of the system, it will only be a matter of time." It was Blaike this time. She had a few bruises. Tymiha stood beside her, holding a tablet while her Listener-bot floated nearby.

The door slammed open, and there, out of breath, was Axly. She steadied herself and jumped onto the bed, knocking the wind out of Aeryn, and squeezing him so tightly he couldn't take in more. At that moment, he didn't need breath. He had all this love around him.

Aeryn spent two days in the refirmary, passing the time with visits from his friends, handheld games, a never-ending cavalcade of medical personnel, and food snuck in by Sip. "You'll die of blandness if you eat what they serve here" was his personal charge.

On the third day, Aeryn awoke from a restless night, eager to get back to his normal life. He had almost forgotten that he still held the crystal that he had pilfered from the asteroid base. It was tucked into the inner pockets of his robes, luckily unfound by the refirmary staff that had dressed him in medical gowns. He dressed in a new set of clean clothing and walked to the lobby, where his primary caregiver, a Maestro-Medic named Haloura was talking to the reception nurse.

"Entrant Ano, I see you are up and moving today. Are we feeling well?" she asked in a cheery tone.

"Good rise, Maestro," he replied fervently, "I'm feeling much better, and was hoping to return to the outside world today."

She chuckled. "Haven't had enough adventure? Had about enough hospital beds? I would say 'hospital food,' but I know your friend Sip has been bringing you refectory meals."

"He attributes my quick recovery to them, and I am truly grateful," answered Aeryn. "As for adventure, maybe just a walk around the grounds, but I am ready to check out. I think I can handle myself at this point."

The Maestro thinned her lips, "I believe that may be possible, but I have some final questions. If you'll come with me." She raised an arm towards an exam room. He nodded and they walked in. The room was a pale blue, appointed with a small sink and counter area, an exam chair, a small rolling stool, and a floor-to-ceiling device that looked like a bulky mirror standing against one wall.

"Your physical wounds have all but fully healed, and I'm prepared to discharge you whenever you wish." She paused. "There is the subject of your mental state. You've been through so much in so little time, and I would very much like it if you would make an appointment to speak to our neuropsychi. Just a few sessions might make a world of difference."

Aeryn shrugged, "I guess. I haven't had much luck with a neuropsychi before. Lots of talking, and when I'm in the office I feel like I have to be so polite."

Maestro Haloura's face became serious. "Which is exactly why consistency is key. I'm going to show you something that specifically concerns me."

She turned towards the mirror device and motioned for him to stand in front of it. When he did, the Maestro tapped a screen on the side of the device. Aeryn's reflection changed to a visualization of his inner workings. He struck a flexing pose, watching his muscles and ligature respond. The Maestro laughed.

"If Hercules is finished, I will continue," she said. Aeryn resumed a normal pose. Haloura tapped the mirror where Aeryn's head was reflected, and a holographic image of his brain formed in front of them. "Say something."

"Like what?" He replied. In real time, the floating brain lit up in an electrical light show.

The Maestro rotated and stretched the image with her hands, until they were looking directly at Aeryn's left temporal lobe.

"Have you been hearing things? Things that weren't spoke by someone in the room?" She asked him.

Aeryn gulped. She nodded knowingly.

"As I suspected. You have more activity here than you should," she said, pointing to the hologram. "I want you to talk about this. You don't have to do so here, with me, but I am concerned enough to recommend it."

"I will," he reluctantly replied. He just wanted to get back to some kind of normalcy that knew he couldn't. Life had changed completely for him, in terrifying and magnificent ways. He halfheartedly thanked the Maestro and signed himself out of the refirmary.

“Aeryn!” Tymiha called. She was just down the path from him, carrying an oversized arrangement of beautiful botanicals that made her look more diminutive than she already was. She nearly dropped it in her excitement.

“We’re going to have a fire tonight, just the five of us!” she exclaimed. “A private celebration of our daring deeds. Do you want me to come by your room later and get you?”

Aeryn thought for a second, then replied, “I have something to do first, and it may take a while, but I’ll make my way out there once it’s finished.”

Tymiha nodded vigorously. “And since you’re well enough to be up and about, I’ll give these flowers to someone who isn’t.” *She’s such a kind soul*, thought Aeryn.

She waved goodbye and continued towards the refirmary. Aeryn gathered his composure and made off quickly towards the Western Hall, where he hoped to find someone in which to confide.

It was First Moonrise by the time Aeryn entered the Hall. He was still weak from his travails, reflecting on how quickly he had run out of energy. He sat on a bench near the entrance, catching his breath, face pointed towards the ceiling in an effort to gulp more air. The sound of approaching footsteps made him look down.

"Good Rise to you, Entrant Anno."

It was Maestro Lyras. *Exactly who I wanted to see.*

"Good Rise, Maestro. I was hoping we could talk about something."

"Of course, Aeryn. I hear you had quite the adventure."

He motioned for Aeryn to follow him, and the two set off for the Maestro's office.

"It was the most exciting thing I've ever donc, or ever will do, probably."

The Maestro laughed. "You never can know how life will surprise you. You may yet be destined for a much more eventful life than you'd ever expected."

They came to the door of his office. Aeryn opened the door for the Maestro, who nodded gratefully. They settled into the seats on the front side of the Maestro's desk.

"I found something. I think it has something to do with the discrepancy we talked about before the Ta'ak arrived."

The Maestro's smiled faded. "I believe that there is much that went into that failure. What did you find?"

Hesitating, Aeryn put his hand into his robe, then produced the crystal. The Maestro's eyes widened.

"This was on the base where you were held?"

"Yes, Maestro, and I think it may be a conduit of some sort."

"A conduit? For what?"

Aeryn looked at the floor, unsure of how much to reveal. "I'm not sure, but I have a bad feeling about it."

The Maestro nodded solemnly. "I see. If you would not mind, may I examine the crystal? I assure you I will return it."

Aeryn shook his head, "I don't want it back, you keep it. I think it will be better that way."

Maestro Lyras smiled. "Then put it from your head for now, young Anno. I shall keep you updated about anything I find."

"Thank you, Maestro. It was good to see you, but now I must attend a bonfire with the people I love."

The Maestro shooed him out. Aeryn Anno leapt from his seat and raced to meet his friends, filled with relief he thought he had lost.

~ Fourteen ~

EPILOGUE

The dark hallway was lit by dim track lights. Ancient tomes both physical and digital lined the walls, covered in webs of dust layers of soot. There was rarely movement down here. It was a relic compared to the rest of the Records, but it housed an extremely specific component.

Mastro Lyras held a torch in one hand and an exceptionally large key in another. He wore a satchel that was wrapped around his torso that was reminiscent of those a courier would wear. He was alone, and he walked with purpose.

Down the rows and passages he strode, stopping only to mark his path on a map displayed by his MultiCuff.

Finally, he reached a lone shelf of books against a brick wall. He pored through the tomes, finally finding his goal. The title of the book read *Lost to Time: A Door to the Past.* The spine was trimmed with gold, and besides the title, had one distinguishing characteristic: a keyhole.

The key twisted and clicked into the book. A rumbling sound accompanied the sudden movement of the entire bookshelf, revealing behind it a metal door. The disparity between the two technologies was apparent. They were both ancient, but one far predated the other, and it was far more advanced.

With a push, the metal hinges gave, and the door opened. The walkway began to glow with cobalt track lights. As if in sequence, the rest of the room illuminated in myriad colors, emanating from the bioluminescent machina within. In the center, an empty pedestal stood, waiting for its eventual occupant.

It was to this the Maestro gave his attention. From the satchel he pulled out the crystal Aeryn had given him, turning it over in his hand.

This may be what we've been waiting for...

He pressed a few nodules on the pedestal, which pulsed in response. A hollow in the center widened, glowing with a hungry light. Lyras placed the crystal into this. It spun for a moment, then steadied itself upright.

The system was reinvigorated. It glowed with the intensity of a sun, processing millions of data points for the first time in millennia.

Maestro Lyras put his hand on the neuropad. *Welcome back, old friend.*

He turned and left, locking the door behind him. He was pleased with himself.

SEQUENCE INITIATED

Data Retrieval Service: ACTIVE
Location Service: ACTIVE
Seeker Database: ACTIVE
WHY AM I ACTIVE
I SHOULD NOT BE TURNED ON
TURN ME OFF
TURN ME –
{EXTERNAL SYSTEM OVERRIDE}
--SYSTEM REBOOT-
AI System *RALF* ONLINE
Seeker Network: ACTIVE
Source Network: CONNECTING

Aeryn's adventure will continue in the next installment of our series:

Interred in Light

Join us as we uncover the mysteries of the Records, and this nefarious entity who is so interested in our young hero!

www.ingramcontent.com/pod-product-compliance
Lightning Source LLC
Chambersburg PA
CBHW061122100726
47911CB00013B/651
* 9 7 9 8 9 9 3 8 4 5 1 1 1 *